CITY OF MANN

CITY OF MANN

L. Ross Coulter

Special thanks to:
Rory, my beautiful wife.
Sadb, my darling daughter.
Larry Contreau
& Prairie (the cat)

Published by Loose Screw Press, 2023
City of Mann
ISBN 978-1-7384407-4-0

Text © L. Ross Coulter
Cover by Loose Screw Press using photography by Kieren Ridley & art
by AI-playground.

The story, all names, characters, and incidents portrayed in this
production are fictitious. No identification with actual persons (living or
deceased), places, buildings, and products is intended or should be
inferred.

To Him who is able to do infinitely more than all we ask or think.

CONTENTS

PROLOGUE

This is not a story of fact.

Instead, it is one of exploration within the limits of imagination, in the search to better understand all that has been given and all that has been seen.

For as it has been said:

> *"As the heavens are higher than the earth, so are my ways higher than your ways and my thoughts higher than your thoughts.*
>
> *For as the rain and the snow come down from heaven and do not return—but instead water the earth, making it bring forth and sprout, giving seed to the sower and bread to the eater—so shall my word be that goes out from my mouth.*
>
> *It shall not return to me empty, but shall accomplish that which I purpose. And it shall succeed in the thing for which I sent it."*

So, as we end, we begin: In the hand of mercy.

THE
CREATION

As with all things that we can comprehend, the start of our story begins at the beginning. And, in the beginning of this story, as indeed with our own, the God who was, and is, and will always be, was already there.

First, creating space from nothing, he filled it with substance. Binding it all to his perfect law, it formed to his command. And vivid and vibrant in its splendor, the universe came to be.

Next, deep in the careful balance of his new cosmic womb, he placed a planet. And as it spun and wobbled on its axis, he molded its mountains and sculpted its shores. Then, binding them too to his perfect law, he drew forth plants and creatures, till the land and the air and the sea swarmed with life.

God provided, and it was good. But all was merely a stage for what came next.

Chapter 1

THE SHAPE OF THE CITIES

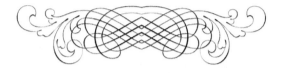

I t was then that God created the Cities.

Sentient, and gifted with an intelligence far surpassing all other life on the planet, they were truly magnificent. And given dominion over all they could see, they were fruitful and multiplied. Till soon, their kind covered their world.

Structure of the Cities

Just as he set laws to hold the planets in their orbits, the birds in the air and the atoms in their attraction, God set laws to govern the physicality of the Cities. Yet the laws of these Cities were quite different to those of the planet Earth.

The mind can conjure up many images when it hears a word, and a word such as 'city' is no exception. A shining metropolis littered with tall glass buildings, or an ancient city of Rome. The parapeted sprawl of a medieval fortress, or maybe the grand gardens and babbling streams of Babylon. So while it would not be wrong in thinking of such places, in the world of the Sentient Cities, the limits of imagination must be tested.

Much as when a human baby is born with two arms and two legs, the basic features of their structures were incontrovertible facts, with all of them sharing basic similarities. So when two mature Cities got together to build a third, it was unheard of that it would turn out any other way, or even, could turn out another way, as they could not even fathom such a thing—let alone have the capacity to build such a peculiarity.

Although somewhat alike to one another, in basic composition they were not too different from your imaginings. Surrounded by high walls, with four large iron gates spaced evenly around its circumference, all were circular in shape, each complete with its own golden temple that sat in the middle. But the first thing you would note to be a little odd, was how they hovered.

Unlike a city in your world that would ordinarily be fixed to the ground, the Sentient Cities were not. Suspended by a force known only to their maker themselves, they floated above the planet's surface, drifting about as they would go about their day.

Much like humans, when a new City was built and it was all but its rudimentary form occupied by a few crude huts, it would stay almost exclusively with its parent Cities until it was a bit older. On reaching a certain age—usually when its basic districts had advanced to building with stone and its barbaric, unintelligible citizens could communicate—it would be sent daily to a gathering of Cities of its own maturity and taught things by the educational class of society to prepare it to navigate the world on its own. So while its parent Cities enjoyed the well deserved peace of its absence, often working to revive the collective fatigue of their populace or sections of their walls that were worn thin, it would develop its knowledge and know-how of self improvement and construction.

As its parent Cities aged and slowly turned to rubble, this would continue for many years. Changing in size and shape, sometimes in the most unseemly manner, the once small, unruly City of simple thatch huts and savages, would grow and grow. Until at last, brimming with glass towers and buzzing with a sophisticated society considered 'adult' amongst Sentient Citykind, it was ready to go out on its own.

It was in this way that the Sentient Cities expanded over the age. Harvesting the rich resources of their planet, moving from riches to riches they thrived. Plants and animals fed their Citizens as metals and minerals paved the way for comfort. And setting their curiosity to task they studied all things large and small. Gifts inside gifts and wealth inside wealth, there seemed no limit to what they could find. So much wonder was hidden in plain sight. Solids to liquids and liquids to gas; the manipulation of matter was only the start. The depth of the wonders of knowledge seemed to extend forever. To copy the shape of an eagle's wing or mimic the lens of its eye! To reproduce the method of the sun's heat, or imitate the rapid firings of a mind! Where there were questions, answers could be found.

So from the creation of all provision, abundance followed. And it was good.

Citizens of the Cities

While the structures of the Cities were indeed a wonder in themselves, they were only one aspect of their totality. For as a body would be without a mind, so would a City be without its Citizens.

Complete in appearance only, without its Citizens, a City would be unable to sustain itself, or even move. No more than a passive thing, it would not be long before it fell into ruin. So, as God created the Cities, he created the Citizens to inhabit them.

If it makes it easier, you may picture them as human. But please, in appearance and basic mannerisms only, as I assure you they are not. Sociable for the most part, they were a friendly creature, somewhat simple as individuals but beautiful in their own way. Quick to act if it was to their benefit, they were lovers of comfort and habit, simultaneously being both wildly unpredictable and stubborn to change. Yet, this was not without purpose. So just as God put laws in place to govern the shape of the Cities' structure, he put laws in place for their people too. And they were good.

Law 1: Free Will

The first of these laws was free will. No matter how much they might ever want to contest it, within the parameters of all the other laws, all Citizens of Cities were free to choose to live in any way that they wished.

This law also applied to their control of the City itself as it roamed the planet, in that, on any given day, if the Citizens decided to have their City spend the day hovering by the sea next to their familial Cities, it would be their choice. And, by that same freedom, if they wished to hurl insults over their walls as they pushed say, a mother-in-law City down a canyon, it would be absolutely within their freedom to do so.

Now, as sense would follow, just because a city *can* do something within the confines of their God-given free will, doesn't mean they *should* do something. It is only reasonable, that going about to do everything within the realms of the possible, will inevitably result in serious harm—or even death. For as water wets and fire burns, the order of reality has been set. And to bend the very fabric of the divine should come with expectation that it will soon come bending back.

What about their safety though? It seems unfair. Shouldn't these things be distinguished for the good of them all?

So they were. And the second law was for them to follow its order.

Law 2: The Constitution

At the creation of the first City, to show the Citizens what things within their free will would send them into trouble, God etched a set of rules on every surface inside its walls. These rules were called the Constitution.

Thinking for a moment that it was etched on some surfaces, you would be right, but a touch naive. As when I say they were etched on *every* surface, I really do mean every surface.

Sitting in a coffee shop, you would see it. First on the wall and then on the table. Again, on your coffee cup, and to your surprise, even on the tip of your shoe! It was everywhere. In fact, the more you looked, the more you would see it. On a road, on a train, on a pen. Even on the saddle of your horse. Written over and over, some in gigantic letters and some so small you had to squint to make out what it said. But nevertheless, it was there, for all to see.

Remember when I mentioned that when two matured Cities would build a new one, it would always turn out like a little version of themselves due to the physical laws?

Yes? Good. Well this same law of replication applied to the Constitution as well, but it was exact. So even when a thousand years had passed and billions of Cities had been built and crumbled, the Constitutional laws in each remained precisely the same. In this way, the tenets of basic order were universal to the Cities understanding. And in this way, all Citizens of all Cities had the truth of right and wrong etched into their very construct.[1]

To see them in action, one would need look no further than a City playground. Hearing the sounds of its infant's cries, a parent City would rush to the aid of their youngster to be told with great confidence of injustice and fairness in a game of tag. And its claim? Right on all accounts! But how did it know? Barely able to convey their outrage, and certainly unable to empty its own sewage system without making a mess, to them, it had been provided.

And it was good.

Law 3: The Collective

It should go without saying, that all laws have implications and results that both benefit and limit certain actions. We would do well to remember though, that with perfect, God-given laws, any perceived limitations should not be viewed as negative things and that a perception of the negative is, in fact, a lack of understanding on our part of the abundant provision that has been made to the contrary. This is no different with the third law; that is, the law of collective citizenship.

Although free to act independently from one another, form families, make friends and join social clubs, all Citizens are

---

1. **Fun fact:** Every unspoken etiquette and legal framework in the history of the Sentient Cities was founded by the laws of the Constitution. From the original '*Global Statutes*' to the '*Charter of Structural Rights*', every amendment and iteration from the beginning of their time sought only to further refine and specify that which was already there since the beginning.
(ISBN 45-02-15)

inextricably bound as a collective unit. Still free of course to make their own choices, the third law connected them to exist as a hive mind, with the actions of the few affecting the many, and the many of the few.

This was achieved by a fluid, almost instant communication from one citizen to another called *nodding*[2] and an agreeableness that was hardwired into each and every one. By and large, this made for Citizens to be a happy, chatty creature. And when walking down any of a City's busy streets it would not be uncommon for the warm sounds and laughter of its Citizens' instant ideas and concurrings to fill the air.

Working as one, it also allowed for them to create extraordinary things which would otherwise be impossible. Out of want, or necessity, a single seed of thought could result in a grand idea, and with every Citizen in the City striving to a common goal, great results could be achieved at incredible speed.

Even from a City's earliest years, the collective workings of its Citizens would rapidly develop within its districts. From the amusements of the Arts & Entertainment center, to the wonders held within the studious halls of the Universities, every Citizen was both part of, and imparted with, each other's participation, growing with the tide of the collective's whim.

It is here, though, that the image of their perfect utopia falls somewhat apart.

---

2. For example: "Yes I agree," she nodded.; or, 'The audience was nodding loudly'; or, 'He nods a lot for someone who says he does not have a lot to nod about.'

Although the third law had many benefits, it was not without quirks, some in and of themselves, and some a consequence of the other laws that preceded it.

As I imagine is common to most, or maybe all collective organisms, one issue was proximity. Unless willing to face quite unpleasant side effects, a single member of the Citizens collective could only stray so far from the group before a serious problem arose. Through many centuries of grisly misfortunes that befell the Cities, it was common knowledge that their Citizens could not survive away from their individual collectives for long and that with much more than a tiny loss of its Citizens[3] a collective could not survive for very long. Whether a high speed collision sending hoards of Citizens careening over the walls, or a physical assault in some sort of City on City altercation, the result was always the same. So to this end, Citizens never strayed beyond the boundaries of their respective City's wall.

Another peculiarity within the limits of the third law, albeit somewhat paradoxical, was an individual Citizen's inability to stay happy for any length of time. Incredible as it was, the speed and agreeableness at which the Citizens communicated with each other

---

3. This was finally proven beyond mere speculation in 11742 by the then renowned, Surgeon City of Jackson. Performing a procedure on a volunteer City under the watchful eyes of several other leading physicians in their fields, he breached the patient's wall and began to encourage its Citizens to leave. Approximately 6 ½ minutes into the experiment, when the number of exiles was approaching 7000, the patient City had permanently lost its ability to hover. Shortly after, the story was leaked by a traumatized medical student, and in the investigation that followed, City of Jackson had his medical license revoked.

did have a drawback. With such enthusiasm did each Citizen communicate, that when one received information from another, it was rarely more than a few seconds before they had blurted it out to whomever was close enough to hear, leaving only enough time for each to add a mere flavor of their individual thoughts or feelings or what it was they were trying to convey. Only the most learned scholars from the best universities could restrain themselves before hurriedly blabbing the news, and even for them it was for no longer than a few short seconds.

This may seem ideal in many ways, as most decisions about almost everything were expanded on, agreed on, and concluded by everybody in the whole City almost instantly—kind of like a supercharged, all-inclusive democracy. But the reality, however, was a little more complicated.

Agreeable and compulsively chatty as they were, Citizens were not designed without a sense of self. Free will, after all, is free will. Like humans, they too had worries and fears, likes and dislikes, needs, and, of course, wants. On an individual basis, in isolation, the problem was not too apparent or problematic. But in the right circumstance, as a collective, it was.[4]

A Monday morning for example, could start as any other, with Citizens preparing for the day of work ahead. But by ten o'clock, of the thousands of conversations that have swept through the entire City in harmony, it would only take one to cause trouble. Let's say a dissatisfied feeling has been voiced from within the Arts & Entertainment district. Other Sentient Cities, it claims, are not allocating as many resources to the Industrial district as theirs, and therefore have more time allocated to culture and relaxation. This is simply not fair, is it not?

Sometimes a dissatisfaction such as this will simply vanish. Relayed from Citizen to Citizen at high speed until it is continually spanning the city, if the general response to it is more disagreeable than agreeable, the collective response counters the dissatisfaction, eventually diluting the dissatisfaction over and over so many times, that soon even the original complainant finds themselves agreeing that the issue was not worth being unhappy about. But although this is ideal, the scenario of diffusion is not always the case.

Coupled with the individual want for itself, the agreeable nature of the collective and the unavoidable fact that Cities interact with many other Cities on a daily basis, chaos is far more common than not. So the same Monday morning with the same dissatisfaction could likely play out like this. . . . .

Convinced that they will never be happy again, by lunch time, every Citizen in the Arts & Entertainment district has gone on strike. Meanwhile, in the rest of the City, a general feeling of dissatisfaction is growing. This slows down optimism and productivity across the board. Soon they refuse to have any input in the City's decisions at all, leaving the Industrial and Educational districts in sole charge of compiling communications to be shouted over the walls to other Cities. Predictably absent of its

---

4. '. . .I find it both unusual and satisfying to work within the field of Citizen Studies. Here I am, no more than a mass of Citizens myself, examining other masses of Citizens and wondering what makes one City's collective sad and another happy. With the benchmark of what makes one happy being perpetually transient and relative to a physicality that ultimately trends to decline, it is no wonder we as a species are inclined to depression.'

- Excerpt from 'City Psychoanalytics Weekly', Edition 498. Article, 'In the Mind of the Collective' by Psychologist City of Trent.

usual elegance or charm, the communication to the other City is not received well at all. And so their response is not only short, but a little rude.

Frustrated by the response received to their rather clumsy communication, the Citizens of the Industrial and Educational districts are the first to express their feelings. As some sob to themselves about their seemingly endless collective shortcomings, others are angry.

"This is the Arts & Entertainment district's fault!" they cry.

Rippling outward across the City, the collective chatter is awash with its outrage, and it is only minutes before their blame reaches the Arts & Entertainment district. And as the Citizens there absorb the news in the mostly agreeable way that they do, the flavor of their nodding turns to guilt.

I will stop here rather than continue on, as I believe you know, or at least can imagine the rest. All that is needed to know is how the day for this City would end.

Unhappy as he hovered home for the evening, the madness of his Citizens would dissipate. Dramatic escalation after dramatic escalation had turned to anarchy among their streets till some even spoke of war. But as had happened many times over, what they held against each other, they soon held against themselves. So by the time the City was ready for bed, he was sad, as he and his people wallowed in mutual self loathing.

What a predicament, you say! What a life! What of their achievements and what of their wealth?! Can they do nothing? Is this how things are to be?! Surely there must be more for these poor Cities?!

And there was. And yes, you have guessed it. It was good. For all provision had already been made.

Rulers of the Cities

Of all the things that were of utmost importance to a City, it was its Temple. Set in the heart of every City, it was magnificent. Ask any Citizen and they would not hesitate to tell you fondly of its beauty.

Climbing a hundred marble steps from the City streets below and crossing beneath the arches of its golden gates, you would first enter its expansive outer courtyard. The air filled with the sounds of agreeable nodding as Citizens of every sort bustle about, your heart would skip a beat in awe at the large stone altar on the raised platform in the center. Past it to the pool of cleansing, you would stop in wonder as you gaze at its pure clear water, until, finally reaching the finale of your visit, you would stand before the Temple itself. Towering above, its marvelous form seems to glow in the sun. Its massive walls of pure white stone, huge golden pillars guard its looming doors. And as you stare up in wide eyed delight, a flock of magnificent birds rises from its roof in a choreographed cloud of flutters.

Yet it is here that you must not go on. For to go any further uninvited means certain death. So taking one last look and heading on your way, you turn your back on the hallowed home of the Temple's prize. The one they call, the Ruler.

In the creation of all things, God's provision was never incomplete. Ruled only by the impulsive whims of their Citizens, meaningful existence for the Cities would be impossible. So in his infinite wisdom, God created for them a Ruler, giving each one dominion over a single City.

The Rulers, it must first be known, were not made of the same matter as a Citizen or a City, or any other matter of the world that they inhabited. Being bound by the laws of known physicality, although coming with many perks,5 has its limitations, and by these the Rulers were not bound.

With eyes that could see through walls and ears that could detect a Citizen's call for help from a hundred miles away, they were given great power in the Cities they ruled.

Immortal, they were set to live forever. Invisible like spirits, they could fly at tremendous speed. Wise beyond their years, they saved, and served, and severed. So feared and revered by the people of their collective, they ruled in fairness to the best of their ability.

But none of this was what made them truly special.

For in his perfect provision, God gave each one of them something utterly unique. A means of hearing him if they listened, and a means of speaking with him if it is what they chose.

After all, God is not simply some higher being who is subordinate to an even higher being, but instead the infinitely high being—for him to provide anything less than himself could not be considered 'perfect' provision. So much as an infinitely perfect6 parent would never leave their young, God did not leave his Cities.

---

5. The 'space race incident', as it was known at the time, very much highlights some of these perks. But in particular, the perk of gravity.

After many years of preparations, it was the Bruushkevs who got the first cosmonaut City, City of Ivan, out of the planet's atmosphere and into orbit. This historic achievement prompted much cheering and celebrations below, yet it was not for nearly twenty minutes that anyone in the control room noticed that he was in trouble. By the time they had pulled on his tether and returned him to the surface it was too late. No longer held by the gravitational perk of the planet, his entire population had floated away and been lost to the depths of space.

He was pronounced dead at 07:09 on 19/209/19039.

6. It was a cold Brexembers morning as the young City of Davinport hovered to school in the snow, accompanied by his aging grandfather.

"Grandpappy," he asked, "My teacher says that the likelihood of a supreme being, being infinitely good, is just as likely as it is to be infinitely bad! How do we know that God is not really a baddy pretending to be a goody?"

"Well," replied his grandfather after a thoughtful pause, "I suppose we only need to look around us to find out."

"Look around? At what?"

"Why at everything, my boy," he chuckled. "If God, being infinite and absolute, was indeed bad—it would make him *infinitely bad and absolutely* bad! That's not just a bit bad, it's as bad as one can be! With *infinite* knowledge and *infinite* power, an infinitely and absolutely bad God would want nothing held in place! No place, no time, no matter would be safe. Everything would be drawn into his eternal chaos!"

"But wouldn't he run out of stuff to be bad to?"

Slowing for a moment to rotate towards his grandson, he gave a loving smile. "You see, you're already beginning to understand? The highest order of anything that can ever possibly exist *has* to be pure, unlimited and everlasting good! For having destroyed everything that had ever been, ever is, and ever would be, a God of infinite badness would be left with only one option. And in its last act, it would be forced to destroy itself."

Taken from the pages of '*Dreams of Days Long Gone*' the biography of Professor City of Davinport, ISBN 05-32-04

Chapter 2

THE WORKINGS OF THE CITIES

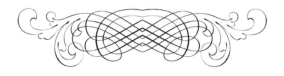

I t is here your understanding of this strange planet has reached its first milestone. Well done. You have learned of its origins, the laws that bind it and the ones for whom it was all made a provision: The Cities—the sentient singularities made of Structure, Citizen and Ruler that inhabit its plains. Yet of how they function and the specifics of their ways, you know nothing.

So I will go on.

Food

For a living thing to survive, its needs must be met. From this, it can be determined, that all living things have needs. While much time could be spent discussing types of need—and time will be given to address such things—the most basic form of a City's need, was energy.

To suspend a City of any size[7] in a state of perpetual hovering requires a great deal of energy. To move a City from place to place requires even more. The same goes for every activity inside of a

City's walls. Whether building a tower block in the business district, repairing or cleaning a section of the outer wall, or simply ensuring that a Citizen has enough energy in their body to get out of bed and perform its job, energy is required for everything. It is in this requirement for energy that we find the need for hunger. And in this hunger, a need for food.

Back when this abstract adventure began if you recall, there was mention of the air, land and sea swarming with life. This was not without purpose. So abundant and complex were these purposes, that grappling to understand them and the myriad of interdependent relationships between them has occupied Scientist Cities for thousands of years. One purpose though, and arguably the best one, was food. The basic premise of 'you have energy and I need energy' exposed.

So if Cities need energy and energy is in food, how does a hovering City get this food?

Why with vacuum tubes, of course, that's how!

For a better understanding of this—and from the perspective of a lowly, yet energy-dense deer—please consider the following:

Munching intently on a particularly green patch of grass, a sound in the distance diverts your attention. Looking up and scanning around the lush and vibrant woodland, the squall of a flock of startled birds confirms your alarm as they rise into the air. Cautious, but eager to continue eating (it's not every day you finds such high-energy grass as this) you resumes where you left off.

---

7. According to Gaitwatchers digest, while an infant City only weighs about 0.92 trillion Kgs, the average adult City weighs in at a whopping 8.23 trillion Kgs (18.14 trillion lb for the numerically stubborn). In the space of only a few hundred years that's a growth of 7.31 trillion Kgs! It's no wonder how a small dietary slip up around the festive season can result in unsightly gains!

Suddenly, a tremor under your hooves lets you know that all is indeed not well. With a crash through the underbrush a bear runs past. Then a worried family of squirrels, and shortly after, a rather out of breath badger.

'Where are you all going?!' you call after them.

But alas, they don't speak deer.

The sound in the sky again, a roar this time! With great certainty now, your fear awakes as the whole earth rumbles. Breaking into a sprint the same way the others went, your heart is beating at an incredible rate. Branches fall from trees and rocks roll down embankments as the mighty sound shakes your world. Not alone by any means, animals of all kinds are doing the same, running and screaming in terror.

Out onto an open clearing that stretches down the valley, you head to take shelter under the closest thicket of trees. But as a great shadow falls across the land you stop, frozen in fear. In bravery perhaps, or maybe a morbid curiosity of who, or what, will consume your energy, you slowly turn in wide-eyed trembling, and staring upward to the heavens, a mighty structure that has all but filled the sky.

Made of rock and earth, as if a mountain scooped from the ground, it is massive in every sense of the word. Blotting out the sun, it spans the horizon, moving slow but steady as it hovers over the earth.

A sight to be seen, it is indeed. With shrieks of chaos and horror it tears through the trees in raging violence, as stretching skyward from its gargantuan form, an enormous vacuum tube howls with ferocious suction. Pulled from their world beneath its awesome guzzle, plants and animals, birds and trees are sent swirling to the craggy underbelly of the great sentient City above.

Nothing is safe. Nothing survives. And as it fast approaches, you thank God for the time you had, and pray for a painless end.

So it was in this manner, you see, that the Cities collected food. With hundreds of these tubes dangling from their undersides as they cruised across land and sea, each and every one was an endless consuming machine, whose harvest scarred the planet in its wake.

The rest was a little less messy. Much more aligned with what you humans are accustomed to, after collection and processing in a City's 'Raw Harvest Facility', various food groups would be distributed to factories before ending up in the aisles of grocery stores. Then, bought and paid for by a City's Citizen, it would be taken home and eaten, where, converted back into usable energy. There they would continue to live, breed and work, completing the cycle of the needs, and thus ensuring the continuation of building, maintenance, and all other works required to keep a City intact.

Resources, Commodities & Specialization

During the rather messy and indiscriminate act of vacuum-tubing, all Cities also gathered resources of the non-food kind. Yet, most not having the particular facilities to process them into more complex commodities, it instead was only fit to trade. This was largely due to the impracticality of having, say, a steel production plant in your City when you only harvested enough iron ore to make one or two tonnes of steel a year. The solution to this of course, was specialization.

You see, as each City was an individual, no two Cities were alike, and even from the youngest age a City would begin to show its interests and disinterests. So if a juvenile City was, for whatever reason, drawn to vacuum-tubing in the same area for long enough until it reached beneath the planet's surface and found raw metal or mineral treasure, it would be a sure sign of what they may one day do as a job.

Beyond the laboring class of Cities, add some education, some time and some effort, and a City could be re-classed; in this case, maybe in the manufacturing class of Cities. Specialization in a sub-class meant a City could manufacture a wide variety of things, from building materials, chemicals, machine parts, plastics, fertilizers, electrical components, papers, pharmaceuticals and much, much more.

By expanding this same process further, the logical introduction of many other specializations becomes apparent. Rather than all Cities producing the physical, some began specializing in producing methods and ideas. Stronger steels and more potent drugs, faster ways to communicate. Specialization gave the ability to every City to advance as an individual as well as lifting up the society of Citykind as a whole. After all, why would you spend your whole day chasing down food to suck up when you could farm it and put it all in one spot?[8] Or hover to a meeting across the country when you can send your voice at high speed through wires? So Citykind progressed. For with every way, there was a new way. And with every new way, a better way.

Mechanics of City Interaction

The implication that Cities can talk to one another having been made several times by now, it would be logical to address how communication between them actually worked. Realizing however, that communication is a secondary function of perception, we will first ask the question of how a City 'sees', or otherwise 'interacts', with the world and Cities around it.

On top of every City's wall there was a walkway that ran the whole way around, complete with fortified battlements. Wide enough for six citizens to stand shoulder to shoulder, in fair weather it was a very lovely place to spend the day. With sprawling views of one's own City on one side and the marvelous expanse of the open world on the other, it was not uncommon to see joggers, families and even tourists from another district ambling about on a sunny day. Apart from the obvious niceties though, it served a very particular purpose. And that was for the work of the Interfacers.

---

8. A distinction should be made to avoid confusion. Familiar as one may be with the dangers of 'fast-food', it is the exact opposite for the sentient Cities. For them, it is 'slow-food' that can be perilous to their health.

From the dawn of Citykind, it did not take much observation to deduce that the food on the planet was fast. Terrified by the sight and sound of an incoming City, all sensible lifeforms would run with much enthusiasm in the opposite direction; meaning that for a City to eat it must move with haste.

Slow-food on the other hand had the opposite effect. Designed for physical comfort and extreme profitability, several bizarre species of animals that were of an unsettling combination of tasty, low in useful energy and utterly fearless were produced. Nicknamed slow-food by their creators at Frankenfood, a subsidiary of CitiCorp, these creatures were quite happy to eat grass and even breed while a City descended upon them. So grouped into large numbers a City could feast for weeks with hardly any movement at all. Unlike the health benefits for a City designed into fast-food, the consumption of 'slow-food' for any extended period resulted in severe structural problems for even the most spry of Cities.

Easy to spot due to their stern gaze and portly physiques, Interfacers were tasked with all of a City's interaction with the outside world. Once ordinary Citizens who had undergone the rigorous training required for the job, they spent their days looking, listening and when commanded, yelling.

Working in shifts and spaced along the wall exactly one hundred meters apart, each would stare intently while listening with their might. If there was anything of interest to note, a quick report made through a little red phone they kept at their posts would relay the information to the command hub. From there, the information would be dispersed amongst the collective Citizens for feedback, and everything working correctly would be followed shortly by the decision of what course of action to take. This could be anything from slowing the City down and changing direction, docking with another City to trade, or, in the case of the need to communicate with another City, commanding the Interfacers on the wall to yell a given message.

Knowing that Citizens cannot leave their City for fear of terrible consequence, you would be prudent to surmise that the visual knowledge of one City to another was limited. Being neither able to see through each other's wall or over each other's wall—bar maybe a cheeky glance at the spire of a tall building—for a City to see inside another's would be like you or I seeing each other's guts, definitely unnecessary and mostly unpleasant. An interaction then, from one sentient City to another, starts with a simple spotting of one another's looming shape on the horizon. If recognition or circumstance prompts further action, the adjustment of trajectory would occur until an appropriate proximity from each other[9] was reached. The blaring noise of thousands of Interfacers arrayed around a City simultaneously yelling 'GOOD DAY TO YOU!', or something similar, would mark that conversation had started. And after a brief pause from the other City while the greeting is received, processed, decided upon and relayed to its own Interfacers, a response would be bellowed back.

Obviously, this simplification disregards the nuanced complexities of social cues, structural language and tonal inflections. But honestly, their communication was not much more than primal screams. Yet it was enough—the primary mechanism by which a thought could be shared and an idea grown from seed. So growth leading to growth, the collective knowledge of the Cities' sentience covered the planet.

---

9. During the industrial revolution of the 19000's, due to the increase in the more densely populated areas and a decrease in 'politeness-education' in the public school system, Cities began to push the boundaries of proximity to a level never before seen in their history. And close-talking became increasingly dangerous.

It should not need to be said, but when several billion tonnes of something bumps into several billion tonnes of something else, it is carnage. Approached by a close-talker, uncomfortable with the hot air, loud volume and spittle that would accompany their conversation, Cities would often reverse in a frantic attempt to widen the gap. Yet, coupled with the problem of population density, this could cause a backward collision with another City.

Known as the close-talking pandemic, this period saw a rise of accidental injury and death to unprecedented levels. And only after his daughter Lucia was crushed under the rear side of his beloved wife in such an incident, did King City of Caspian IV set into law the 'Minimum Distance Act' of 19328 that brought it to an end.

The first of its kind, this law still stands as legal precedent today and is considered the gold standard of the personal space laws.

THE CITY OF MANN

Much as a fruit cannot exist without first the existence of a branch for it to be formed from, can an idea be developed without ideas from which to grow, or knowledge be gained without knowledge for it to expand from.

In this way, dear reader, we have reached this moment. For to launch a story of a sentient City on its own would be madness. Yet, in this moment, it may actually make a little sense. So while there is much more that could be said on their species and their world, their history and their purpose, a foundation has been laid.

And on this, we[10] can begin to build.

---

10. "But who are we, you and I?! Are we the same? By no means! We are different! Bred for different plates, we are brown and we are white! Crosshatched for different tastes we are scored left and right! Of course we are different! But is this the reason for hate?! For are we not all the same? Whether grain or wheat, was it not from the ground our substance came? Whether like or unlike, one steamed and another baked, were we not all shaped by the Baker? It is not by one hand we have been created? So I say to you my friends—We are not friends!—We are more!! We, my brothers and sisters, in creation we are one! And by His almighty hand, we are Kin!!!"

— *The call to love by Générale Bâtard, from 'The War for Bastion Bakery'* (ISBN 45-09-03)

Chapter 3

THE WORLD AT THE TIME

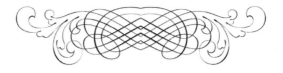

In the thousands of years that had passed since the first Sentient City, the world had become a very different place. As if reaching its very limits, centuries of imagination probed in every direction[11] and innovation and invention seemed to know no bounds. Science and Business, Law and the Arts; every field of study and topic of interest expanded minds and paved the way for a brighter future.

With ideas came methods, and with methods came machines. Big ones, small ones, smart ones and shiny ones. One to solve a task and another to tackle a topic. The world of the Cities hummed with their power and the flow of knowledge ran free to whomever it was wished.

This is not to say that it had all gone well. History had shown an unpredictable pattern of predictable suffering. Time and time again, war, famine, disease (don't be silly, of course they can get sick) and a host of other problems had plagued the Cities, molding country and culture in its unstoppable tirade. Fortunately though, times such as these did not last forever, and in the times between, the Cities regrew and rebuilt, always hungering in the search for more.

---

11. "Beyond our imagination?" he scoffed. "Foolish girl. Imagination is limitless. What such a place do you imagine could be beyond that?"

Composing her anger, she looked up at him with stern glare, being careful not to speak so loudly as to disturb the other passengers. "Mister Rothington!" she hissed. "I would kindly insist that you never speak to me like that again! And although I do respect your opinion, I cannot say the same for your arrogance! If so boundless— tell me—what is the most unimaginable thing that your limitless vision can muster? What inexplicable shape or incomprehensible matter? Or is it so odd that it can only be expressed in mathematical form? Please, I am eager to hear."

An uncomfortable silence lingered broken only by the rattle of the tracks beneath the carriage as Mister Rothington opened his mouth to answer, but then stopped and fell quietly into thought.

"My apologies Miss Portsmith," he continued after some time. "I realize that if I describe anything at all to you in any way, you will have proven me wrong, will you not? I should not have spoken to you in such a way, or indeed have spoken with such authority without giving such a matter my deeper thought."

"No apologies necessary," she replied, feeling sheepish for her outburst. "My intent was not to prove you wrong, only to show you the outer edges of our imagination where even in its most abstract of forms we are bound by the limits our perception."

"So beyond our imagination then," he said, his eyes twinkling with a hint of a smile. "How do you propose we get there?"

Shuffling her feet she looked at the floor. "Hope, Mister Rothington. Hope."

Taken from 'Lady Battersby Goes to Lunch'
by A.M. Canoodle
(ISBN 46-02-09)

Chapter 4

THE BIRTH OF THE CITY OF MANN

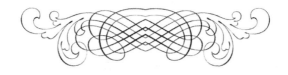

Upon reaching structural maturity, any two Cities of the appropriate construction may choose to band together and create another City. This is encouraged in Sentient City society as it is the only way of continuing their species, as well as being a thoroughly amusing process for both parties concerned.

Lining up their southern gates, partnered Cities will dock with each other for a short period of time, allowing for the transfer of Citizens from the building school in one, to the specialized construction facility in the other. On arrival, these Citizens, trained in a variety of building and design disciplines meet with a team of experts in the same field, and together, after many boardroom meetings, contractual negotiations and signing on dotted lines, the production of a new City will begin.

In the eight years it takes to build a small City, while the City who is undertaking the internal construction of the new City vacuums up a tremendous amount of matter to support the building process, the other does its best to provide additional support and resources until the day of offloading.

When the time arrives, the infant City is lifted by a massive gantry crane to the southgate, and with much arguing between the designers and builders on who did the final measurements of the City and the gate itself, which was clearly not coordinated, the new City is pushed out and lowered onto the surface of the planet for its first time.

In this way, Mann was made. And in the traditional way, as Ruler of the new City, the new City he ruled was called City of Mann.

Ruling, from the start, was not an easy job. Bear in mind that his Citizens had not yet advanced past the primitive stage and their buildings were only huts. Orchestrating even a simple act like vacuum tubing or a sewage system jettison was far from easy. Flying across his City to rally them to action was in itself of immense difficulty. To them, he was quite terrifying.

Appearing as no more than a voice, his commands and encouragements in the beginning did little more than scare them away. But as time went on, first one, then many, slowly started to heed his word. And determined to help them grow, he pushed and guided and led.

Bit by bit, they began to learn. Reading, the words of the Constitution etched in the City walls and streets brought about the advent of order. And writing—shaky at first—practice made perfect, and their newfound civility gave way to everything else. Covering their bare bottoms with crude garments and fashioning tools to help them work, they soon mastered the basic operations of the City infrastructure. And hailing Ruler Mann as their guide and their god and their king, they did not stop there.

As any ordinary City did, City of Mann grew up in the ordinary way on the outside too. His first word, although not much different than his Interfacers' usual babbling and screaming, was 'Cat'. His first solid food was the fringes of a delicious boreal forest and, younger than average, his first wobbly hover was taken when he was only two hundred and seventy six months old.[12] What a sight it was. His parent Cities were so proud. Bolstered by their cheers, he sputtered with energy and lifted off the planet's surface all by himself. Concentration at maximum, he focused on their shapes and the sounds of their acclaim.

"Almost there!", they shouted as he cleared the first mile. "You can do it! Just a little further!"

But with a sudden trip it was all over. Veering sideways in an uncontrolled fumble, a mountainside took the brunt of his fall. For a moment, as the destruction of thousands of habitats and the ecosystem that supports them rumbled in the air, he thought he had failed. Yet, as his parent Cities approached and he heard the delight in their tone, he knew he had done well.

Everything else was usual too. Third out of four siblings, he had two sisters and a brother. City of Erin, the eldest. Then Ann, and lastly, Julian, the baby of the family. Sometimes, due to the unfortunate rhyming of Sister City of Ann's name and his and

---

12. For the Sentient Cities, the adaptation of a parent City to the use of time's higher denomination of measurement when referring to their child's age—that is, years instead of months—typically occurs between 138 months (11.5 years) and 276 months old (23 years).
In some instances, particularly where one or both of the parent City's mathematical studies buildings has fallen into disrepair or been damaged, this can be a lot higher, with the age of some infant Cities still being referred to in months in their 60's!

their notably different temperament (she was quite boisterous in comparison), he would get overlooked or misheard. Otherwise, it was also all quite ordinary. Schooling had commenced at the customary age, and concluded some years later with nothing much to note. So saying farewell to his parents only a few days after his five hundredth and second birthday, he made the long trip to the metropolis of Epicurea on the western coast of the Ataraxian peninsula.

In the eyes of Citykind and the World that they lived, he had matured.

Chapter 5

THE PLANET PROVIDES

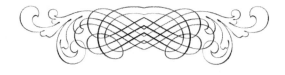

Epicurea was a wonderful place. Filled with ambition and success, it was a sensory feast of every idea and discovery provided in every age. A pinnacle of the Sentient Cities' achievements, its epic proportions hummed day and night with its endless goings on. Unlike where City of Mann had grown up, all the paths were paved. Instead of winding across the plains and valleys on the trails made from the to-ing and fro-ing of Cities over the years, they were perfectly straight, and wide enough for two of even the largest Cities to pass. Stretching out as far as one could see, they were laid out in a grid that formed square plots of land between them, with each square having a designated purpose. Apartment blocks, offices, and shops. Eateries of every kind. All bustling with a multitude of his sentient kin. So many, in fact, that there he saw more Cities in a day than he did in a whole year back home.

It was all such a thrill. Even the short journey to his new job was exciting. Hovering at full speed down one of the beautifully straight paths, he would yell hello at every City as they zoomed past him in the other lane.[13] Past the rivers and vegetable fields of

---

13. It may not be immediately obvious what a novelty a paved road is to the average City.

Due to the enormous cost of paving a path the width of a City, let alone two side by side, nearly 90% of all the paths on the planet were unpaved and single lane. This meant that in their lifetime, most Cities would never pass another at any speed at all.

You see, outside of the Metropolitan areas, where there was no reasonable room to travel 'off-path' for a time, such as a gorge or valley, two Cities heading in opposite directions were legally obligated to comply with what was colloquially known as the 'After You' procedure. This was because, as we have noted before, Cities, being Cities, were of tremendous weight and size, so the sheer destruction of a collision of any sort was often life changing for everyone involved.

How it worked was, that the first City to spot another coming towards it must declare at the top of its voice, "*After you!*" and, after reducing its speed to a full stop, hover off the path until the other City has passed safely by. This elegant solution however, was not perfect, as it did not take into account two key factors common to Citykind;

Lateness and Politeness.

Lateness: When a City was running late, the terribly tempting decision would arise as they approached another to say nothing, pretending instead that they had not seen anyone in the hope that they would gain the right of way to keep going. Illegal maybe, but who would know? Sooner or later the oncoming City would have to say 'After You', and they would be on their merry way. This was, until rush hour. While one late City could be rude, two late Cities could be deadly. And if both were over committed to not being late, the consequences were dire.

Politeness: Although perfectly lovely behavior in itself, the issue with politeness was that after hearing an, 'After You,' for example from an approaching City, one might think it nice or proper to say, 'No, good Sir, After You', and come to a stop. It was. Yet if two Cities of equal politeness came face to face, then a dangerous dance of manners began. 'After you,' one would say to the reply of, 'Not at all, after You.' And then, 'But please, I insist,' to, 'No, good sir. After you.'

Back and forth in a repetitive, and increasingly frustrating loop, this could go on for hours or even days, as both Cities awkwardly and painfully tried to circumnavigate the other. Less deadly than its counterpart and usually only the cause of traffic jams, politeness too if left unchecked could cause injury, death, and even economic collapse as what happened during the Great Traffic Jam of 28343.

the local vegan cafe he would cross the intersection where a line of Cities waited for the traffic lights to change. Reaching the billboard out front of PastureLand that read, 'Livestock from three different continents!!' he would look in with envy, as hungry diners vacuumed up the special of the day. And as he continued on his way, the sound of jubilee floated through the air from behind the fence of the disco next door, to where, peeking past the bouncer City to the asphalt surface of the dance floor, Cities of all kinds spun and frolicked in carefree merriment.

With a head full of eager anticipation of the coming weekend, he would reach his workplace at the Epicurean branch of CitiCorp international. Much resembling one of the many beautiful multistorey car parks of Earth, it was an impressive thirty something floors of neat offices, meeting rooms and relaxation areas. And he liked it there.

Comprised of ramps, platforms and open work spaces where Cities could freely mingle, think and share ideas, it buzzed with an energy he had never felt before. There he felt alive and purposeful, and for the first time, part of something bigger. The Cities that worked there were different, well spoken and fashionably decorated they exuded charm and confidence as they hovered about their business.

Young and old, refined and ambitious. Always striving for more and never settling for less. Hungry for great change and thirsty for great things. They were the Citykind he had read about in books and been taught about in history class and CitiCorp was their shining vessel. They were the innovators and the creators. They were what Cities were made to be. Never moving in the staleness of the lateral, but onwards and upwards! Paving the way for CityKind to discover its perfected self!

Chapter 6

LIFE AMONGST THE OTHER CITIES

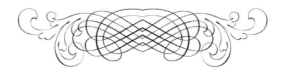

I n the world amongst the other Cities, City of Mann learned
fast. All was such a thrill, but becoming quickly aware of
himself in the eyes of others, he knew he had to change. First
resurfacing his outer walls in a blemish free render, he garnished
himself in paints from the latest trends. A smart charcoal wash for
his facade and an oxford white trim to accentuate the details of his
parapets, he finished it off with a semi-gloss navy for his gates.

Beyond that, and not mentioning his new, and much stricter
structural maintenance regime, there was extensive work to be
done on the inside of his walls as well.

His Citizens with their fanciful ideas; their collective thoughts
so simple and unrefined! If the other Cities found out what they
were really like!! Oh, how they would laugh!

And his Interfacers! What an embarrassment! Even the rare
time when his Citizens provided them with coherent feedback,

they would undoubtedly choke, yelling messages with such stutter and tone as to bring quizzical glances and murmurs of mockery.

But despite humiliation at a meeting, or the time he was laughed at during a formal lunch,[14] Mann was determined,

---

14. **CitiCorp International - Accident Report - D167**
Date/time of incident: Wodsemper 48th, 29435 at 14:09
Location of incident: Chubby City Bar & Lounge, 39 Wallsworth St. Epicurea
Name/Title of employee involved: Intern City of Mann
Report written by/filed by: Senior Partner City of Babbage
Description of incident: During our bi-annual team building luncheon in accordance with company policy #108, my team and I entered the restaurant and took our places around the vacuuming table I had booked some days earlier. City of Mann, a relatively new intern with the company, occupied the place directly opposite from me. I could see from the start that he was uncomfortable, as, in addition to an unholy amount of moisture condensing on his upper walls, he was laughing rather too loudly at jokes and chiming in with other conversations at inopportune times. This is not unusual for new employees so I thought nothing of it at the time. It was only after the Waiter Cities had loaded up the table with food, that I realized that City of Mann knew nothing of forward-feeding. It was then that the incident occurred.

As the rest of us, including several other senior partners, began to extend our vacuum tubes forward to reach the various foods, the most tremendous noise of City of Mann's hovernodes going into overdrive signaled that something was wrong. Elevating himself to the height of the table he began to vacuum as he hovered right onto its surface. But by the time he realized his error it was too late. Sliding backwards as the table tipped under his enormous weight, everyone yelled in horror as their food slid towards him at terrible speed, and as he crashed back onto the ground he and our team were covered in it from battlement to base.

Remedial action: The restaurant was compensated for the inconvenience and for the structural damage to the premises caused by the fall. Citicorp employee induction process has been updated to include a mandatory eloquence assessment session with HR prior to assimilation with full-time workforce.
Signed: *City of Babbage*

defiant. He knew he could do better. Maybe his City and his Citizens and his Interfacers were not the best—but they could be! He was made for more, he was meant to be more; he could feel it! Just a little more time, a little more work. But one could hardly expect to overcome the world without first absorbing the standards of its finest!

So he worked. And the Great Adaptation began.

His Interfacers were the first to be changed. Tearing down their old Academy at his command, a new was built. Bigger, better, and fit for the times, the candid unsophistication of their past was recast by the motto wrought above its shining gates: 'Mirror and Conceal'.

There, his interfacers would learn the language of the modern City, and there the transformation of his being would be born.

His Citizens too! A change of half measures would not amount. To reach the potential of Citykind, every man, woman and child of his great City would need to move as one, act as one and grow as one. So setting them to task, they built on a scale never seen before.

Universities and libraries to expand the galaxy of the mind. Galleries and museums for the majesty of the Arts and Culture. Programs and projects of every sort. Knowledge to strengthen and entertainment to invigorate and reward!

"Onwards and upwards my beautiful Citizens! Together!" he praised them as they busied about their work. "Together! We must adapt or die!!"

The Rise of Politicians

Mann did not remember when, exactly, the first Politician was appointed by the Citizens. Or the second. In fact, for as long as he could remember his Citizens had always appointed Politicians to vocalize their needs. Someone cut from their cloth to listen to them and speak on their behalf. By the time of the Great Adaptation, there were already dozens. Queens and Kings, Lords and Ladies, Duchesses and Dukes. All vying for his attention and that of his people.

He was not naive to the challenge this posed, but how else would it work? There were far too many Citizens with far too many feelings for Mann to address each one. Even at a young age he would spend hours addressing the tears of a group, only to hear the cries of 'neglect!' from the rest. And that was when his City was all but mud huts and thatched roofs. Problems in those days were easy. The collective wail of hunger or the simultaneous outrage of another Infant City's indiscretion were the extent of his worries. But those days were gone. His City and his people had grown so much since then. Now numbering in the millions, their advancement in collective thought had brought forth new challenges. Basic needs of nourishment and safety were no longer simple; contemplation of the world past the city walls had seen to that.

Of course, the expansion of knowledge of the big wide world beyond the City walls did come with hope and optimism, but it also came with fear, and with fear came the hunger for more. So as the hunger for the needs of today were met, they turned quickly to the hope of the same for tomorrow. And when the hope of tomorrow was satisfied, they looked to the day after that, and then the one after that. More and more and more, until the object of their hunger became not the object itself, but the 'more' upon which it was satiated. All of which were but a prelude to the need of worth and belonging. To feed a seed is to awaken root and branch is it not?

So, "Who are we and what is our worth?" they asked themselves. "What makes us of value, and to whom? Are we loved then? Are we lovable?"

From answer to endless answer, the questions of continuous doubt were unceasing. For Mann to listen to and answer them alone would have been impossible. With only so many hours in a day and already so much work to be done, it could not be achieved. So the Politicians were the way out. A necessary order and a personification of his people's needs.

On any given day you would find a politician in one of two places: out amongst the Citizens who voted them in, or in the Temple.

Among the Citizens, they would spend their time addressing concerns, countering them with the comfort and reassurance that no voice will go unheard. In the Temple, when not in their chambers, they would assemble in the Hall of Sanctum, unleashing clever diatribes upon one another until it was time for the Grand Assembly of the Council. Where, with Ruler Mann himself in attendance, they would let their real games begin.

Mann hated the Assembly and the torturous labyrinth of words that it could often be, but knew of the necessity of its occurrence. Taking his seat on the podium, he would take stock of the semicircular array of Politicians and dignitaries before clearing his throat to let them know that the meeting was to begin. (Do not forget that Mann, as all Rulers, was quite invisible, so this procedural throat clearing also served the secondary function of alerting the Assembly members that he was there.) Once the usual announcements were done with and the meeting was underway, Politician after Politician would present their cases and he would listen, responding as best as he could to try and keep the peace.

Was it easy? No. Was it fun? Absolutely not. But it served its purpose. All the needs of the City of Mann and its Citizens addressed in only a few long hours.

A worry about raw materials from his Industrial district put to rest, saved a workers strike. Panic over rumors from outside the walls of layoffs at CitiCorp quenched, stopped a riot. A call for war against another City in retaliation to a nasty email snuffed before it spread too far. The Politicians said their piece and Mann answered. Soothing nerves and tempers with careful concession and dangling compromise for the greater good.

Yet he always thought it strange. For as much as they asked and for as much as he answered, he knew that whatever he did would inevitably not be enough.

Of food to feed the City, he said let us find food. Of safety, shelter, friends and wealth—let us work. Let us love, he declared, let us belong. Let us do what we must to have what we need. Let the other Cities see what we want them to see. Let them see what we are, what we're worth and what we can do!

But generation after generation as his Citizens had come and gone, and the limits of their needs and questions seemed as if they had no end, no-one had asked the bigger question. The culmination of all their hopes and desires and fears. The question at the end of it all. Beyond the world inside the walls of their crumbling City, was there more?

If you would please, take a moment to do a simple thing.

Hold out your fleshy hand in front of your face. What do you see? It is you, is it not?

Now, poke it with your other hand and squish a bit of its squishy skin. Wiggle its appendages. If it is you—which it is— what then, is the you that is looking at it and telling it to wiggle.

It is not your eyes, no. Those are also things by which you function. Your brain then, yes? Yes, it must be your brain that sees your hand and wiggles your fingers. Questioning itself, contemplating itself and giving you an odd sense of detachment from the meaty frame that you operate, it is the collective matter of your brain that forms ideas about its purpose.

So what then, of purpose? Eyes to see hands and hands to perform work, both in contribution to the body's collective provision for the brain. But what does the brain provide for? Is it, in its unparalleled complexity, intended as mere food for the earth? **15** Its matchless consciousness lost to dust. Is it but the meaningless climax of an almost incalculable number of dependent provisions? Or is there more?

Mann felt much the same about his City. Although he had never known anything else, perceiving the outside world through the account of his Interfacer's observations was an unusual experience. Relayed to him in a timely and accurate manner, what they saw and heard was what he saw and heard, and with the exception of his occasional trip to the top of the walls he had learned to greatly trust their factual accounts. But unlike his younger years where he liaised with them directly, the times had changed. These days, information from the outside rarely reached him directly without due process. Filtered through the multitudes of his Citizens, it was only after it was distributed and directed to the appropriate districts for detailed analysis, that it would finally be relayed to him by the Politicians. So when a report came of a yeast infected vacuum tube or damage to his outer wall, it was not without personal concern, but he just couldn't help but feel a little disconnected. His City with its walls and buildings and functions were him, yet somehow, they were not.

His Citizens too. They were like family, closer even. They were of him. In a way, they were him. He had known their grandparents, and their grandparents before that. He had seen them all at birth and heard all their cries. They were the ones on which every growth of his conscious self was built, yet still, having never really seen him and often not even knowing he was there, they were not him. And in those starry nights when they huddled in their beds with their own, he would wonder what was to become of him when they were gone.

15.

Empathetic Extremists Weekly - Issue #379.
(Excerpt from, *'Feeling Around the Forest Floor'* by Karl
Bermenthall)
(ISBN 43-12-24)

"Please, my dear sweet Acorn, lying there amongst the leaves—do not be sad. Your despondence is for naught! If only you could see! It is not that you have no purpose and no future; yours is just of a glory of such magnificence that its very premise dances beyond the fringe of your imagination. If only I could show you what you would become! Do you think that you are so different from the rest of creation, that every prior occurrence in the gargantuan expanse of the surrounding universe exists to sustain you to end without purpose? That the myriad of minuscule interactions between the atoms and molecules that conspired for your being, occurred to snuff you out without reason? Is your smooth green body and rough brown base the focal point of everything else? Of course not. It too has a place in the graceful symphony of interconnected provision. Not just to rot. Death is only the beginning! A momentary eclipse! Free from your nutty form you can transcend to the sky with trunk and branch and leaf. Mightier than the mightiest creature in the woods you will be reborn! So do not lose heart my little one! Do not give up! And strive! Strive to receive the best patch of dirt and the freshest drops of rain! Strive to never lose hope and never be lost by it! And hope will never let you go. As hope is that glimmer of light that shines through the canopy for you."

Accidents, Ailments & Disasters

City of Mann was not weepy or leaky like humans. This was not a feature exclusive to him, but rather a wondrous mercy extended to all of the Great[16] Sentient Cities. He was, however, still susceptible to the wear and tear that relentlessly battered the life on his planet.

'Wear', of course, was none other than the classic way of age, while 'tear' was the reminder that wear had by no means gone away. And as did everything under the sun, they too had purpose.

On his planet, it was a rule that all things must die. Yet, for all its unavoidable certainty, it was an unspoken rule that was mostly swept under the rug. City of Mann had first noticed this at the passing (to Citykind, this word means death; she died and stayed dead) of his Great Aunt City of Clara.

At the service held for her friends and family, Cities said such strange things. Many told him that they were sorry. This confused him. What exactly did they mean? Were they somehow responsible? How was it that so many of them were involved?

His Cousin City later explained that this was not the case. They were not at fault. Instead, they were sorry for his loss. This made a bit more sense, and was nice, but a bit short sighted. He had already pontificated the outcomes if she never died, and not a single version of his imaginings ended well at all. There was the version that she did not go to Gobbledy Gorge that day and the one that she fell but survived. But while both did the trick in the moment, eventually she always ended up in the same place. Dead. And what was so wrong with that? She had done exactly what she had been destined to do since birth. In fact, by his estimation it was the only thing she would definitely do yet the achievement was only muttered in a whisper.

It was not that he didn't care either, or not understand why one would be sad—it was sad. He loved his Aunt very much and missed her already. And he felt so sorry for his Great Uncle City of Cecil who must have missed her a great deal more, that when he got home he cried and cried and cried.

But he just didn't quite understand everyone else. How they acted and how they talked about the inevitable end. The words they used were so strange. As if they would prefer it to not exist, they would hide its presence in riddles and half truths. And the more he thought about it the more it bothered him.

---

16. **Fun fact:** The word '*Great*', in 'Great Sentient Cities', is indicative of Sentient Citykind's position on the 'Intergalactic Status of Species Schedule'.

Introduced by CASA (the City Aeronautics and Space Administration) in 13892, the schedule had a scaled range from 'Terrible' to 'Great' that was to be used to classify other sentient species, (if ever found) based on their appearance, social prowess and bodily function (or lack thereof.)

This was brought into being after it was discovered that an interaction between a City who considered itself 3 status-points or more than another, almost always induced disgust in the higher statused City, due to the phenomenon known as '*down-nosing*' that shows a correlation between one's perceived status in relation to another's, and disgust.

If, therefore, the Sentient Cities ever discovered alien life of a different status, CASA concluded that this same reaction would be highly likely and could potentially lead to an intergalactic conflict. After much consideration, the Sentient Cities Council of War determined to assign the Sentient Cities the highest title on the schedule and in 13898 it became law. Ensuring moral superiority over any intergalactic visitors that may arrive, the 'Great' Sentient Cities would be free to befriend or enslave as they wished, thus ensuring freedom from tyranny for them all.

Grandmother City was next to go. Dramatically ejecting her false vacuum tubes as she crashed to the ground to the surprise of a horrified crowd, a massive failure of her power plant killed her dead while out shopping.

"Passed where?" he had asked, as he looked into the grave to which her enormous structure had been shoveled. "What's down there?"

The answer was strange. "Not down there," he was told, "up there. In heaven."

Craning their necks upwards for some time, his interfacers confirmed that there was nothing but sky above them and peering downwards again, he confirmed too that his dear Grandmother City was still very much at the bottom of the hole. "She is not," he replied. "She's down there. Look."

The condescending laugh of one more arrogant than another followed, "No silly! That down there is just her empty City. The real Grandma has flown away."

"Oh." The general feeling of his citizens was quite perturbed. "I didn't know one could? So before all of this then. . . she was stuck? Am I stuck?"

"No, not stuck. Not exactly. Where you are right now is where you are supposed to be, but when the time comes you will fly away too."

This was not a satisfactory answer to his question and as time raised the depths of his thoughts he had many more. He appreciated the earnest answers, most of them anyway. But to every answer he got, he had a question. Flying spirits? Heaven's and hell's? A God, or three!?—Or maybe none? Some said it was one way and others said it was not. How could they all be right?

So the question remained the same. But it was never quiet. And the accident that took Aunt Clara and the ailment that took Grandma was only the start.

"Do you think they were ready?" he asked, as the live footage of the tsunami playing on the screen showed scores of Cities being swept to their deaths.

"For what?" his father City answered. "That? I can't imagine anyone would be ready for that! But don't you worry—things like that will never happen around here. We're much too far from the ocean."

"No, not that in particular. I mean the end. You know, when they—"

"Oh dear boy!" he scoffed, "You needn't worry about that either. There's more than enough to do in getting ready for tomorrow. Why, if we spent every day thinking about all that, we'd never get anything done!"

"No. I suppose we wouldn't. It just seems strange, that's all. Caring so much about what *might* happen, over what *will* happen just seems a bit backwards. I just wonder if perhaps we are looking at it wrong. Are we not supposed to die?"

"My sweet boy! How splendidly glum! Where do you get such ideas! Come on, enough television for you I think—off to bed with you!"

By the time City of Mann moved to Epicurea, he had been taught well. Immersed in years of delightful vaguery and masterful sidestepping, he and his Citizens had learned so much in the art of concise avoidance, that most of any instances that broached his definite demise were waived away with a similar ease.

'I'm so sorry,' became his line at funerals.

'It's just the saddest thing,' did the trick for world news.

Was it that he didn't care? No, not at all. In fact, deep, deep down, he cared so much it hurt. But he was terrified.

Like when his Friend City of Bobby, lost his brother. The funeral was on a Tuesday out in the Weston burial plains. It was raining and City of Mann watched from the back of the crowd. He did not want to be a nuisance, the family had enough to worry about. So he waited.

Wise words by a Priest City were followed by a few tales of happier times. And then, as a young relative City struck a melancholic solo, singing the words; *'We built this City—We built this City, on roccck and roll'*, four large attendant Cities shoved the empty carcass of the deceased into the hole.

After the gigantic cloud of dust cleared, the crowd thinned and City of Mann went graveside to where his friend hovered by himself. He had planned on saying something wise, topped off with a joke to keep it light. Yet the moment his Interfacers saw those of his friend they fell silent.

There are rare moments in the life of a Sentient City where its Interfacers report a code red.[17] Mann was in the Temple when he heard of it.

"A red!!" he exclaimed, startling the politicians in his vicinity with his invisible outburst. "It can't be!"

The highest of all of the codes, code red was also the quietest. So as he rushed outside, he knew it was real. The courtyard was silent, and as he shot through the gates, so were the streets. His Citizens were still there—still everywhere—but they barely moved, nodding only in the softest whisper as they looked nervously to the sky.

"It is all going to be fine, little ones!" he called out to them as he hurtled over their heads. "Just hang on! Everything is all going to be alright!"

17.

The Practical Interfacer's Guide to Effective Interfacing (Third edition)

Chapter 8: Emergency protocols; *'When the room reads you'*

There are three types of emergency codes that are an essential part of an effective Interfacer's toolkit. The distinction of each is of utmost importance and must be committed to memory. (This is a mandatory requirement for any Interfacer wishing to graduate and will appear in the final exam.)

CODE YELLOW: A personal crisis. Externally presenting as awkward gaps in conversation and/or unfunny or stupid verbal outbursts, it is typically caused when the Collective Citizens of a City get caught in a loop of self questioning, guessing or loathing. The most common type of emergency, it is most often triggered by uneasy situations, e.g. a first day of work; conversing with a City that is notably cooler/hipper than oneself; mistakenly asking a City of ample proportions when their infant is due.

CODE BLUE: A physical crisis. Externally presenting as shouts, screams, cries or even a complete shutdown of outward communication, it is typically caused when the Collective Citizens of a City get caught in a loop of terror. This can be triggered during or after:

A.) Physical damage to the City (Lacerated walls, Infrastructural ruptures, Structural breaks, etc.)

B.) Widespread physical damage to the Citizens (Fire, flood, plague, chemical spills, etc.)

C.) Widespread psychological damage to the Citizens (Harmful ideas, depressing thoughts, etc.)

CODE RED: An existential crisis. Externally presenting as silence, it is typically caused when the Collective Citizens of a City get caught in a loop of purposelessness, meaninglessness or faced with decisions/events so great that the collective ceases to function. It can also be caused by an untreated code blue and can be triggered by things that highlight the inescapable reality of death (e.g. Sickness, injury, world news, funerals, loss of a family member) or an incident such as moving in with one's in-law Cities.

Important note: The Spirit Ruler must be notified immediately of a code Blue or Red. A code Yellow is to be reported at the end of each 24 hour period unless more than 3 have occurred within this period. (3 or more code yellows is often symptomatic of an oncoming code blue.)

Reaching the top of the City walls, his Interfacers stared at him pale faced as he arrived.

"Our deepest apologies, my Lord!" they said, "The Citizen's Collective has gone into shutdown! We have no direction of what to say!! They just keep asking the Question, over and over!"

"The Question?!! Why?!" he replied. "The funeral was going so well! What happened?!"

"That did," they replied, simultaneously pointing over the parapet.

Following their pallid gaze, the sight of City of Bobby cut like a knife. His Interfacer's eyes were red. Tears streamed down their cheeks. Trying to wail but maybe too tired to try, all they could seem to do was shudder with labored breaths. Seeing them, he could only imagine what a hell of grief and fear it must be like in the City. Maybe a code blue and a red at the same time?! And then he saw Bobby. Not the City of Bobby—although he could of course see him too—but Bobby the Spirit Ruler. Flying back and forth on his City battlements, howling in torment and sobbing like a child.

Mann's heart ached for his friend. He understood in part. He knew what it was like to be burdened with the rule of a City. To be known but never seen. One with your Citizens, your flesh, your kin—but somehow apart. But he didn't understand it all. How could he? No one can ever know the full weight of another's pain or the depth of their scars. Their anguish and fear, and shame and regret. No one. And as he heard Bobby's bleating cries carry through the air, he felt his terror of the Question that must be cutting through his existence like a razored blade. Where did his beloved brother go?

"My Lord?!" the frantic shouts of Mann's Interfacers snapped him from his trance. "Lord Mann!! Please!! What are your orders?!!"

"What?! I—" Mann stuttered, haunted by his burning sorrow for his friend. "I don't know, we—we must go on!"

"But Sire! What about the Question?! The Citizens are panicking!!"

The urgency in their voices was shrill in his ears. He knew they wanted to know—they had a right to know, an imperative to know! But he didn't know. So he did all he knew how.

"Shut it down!" he commanded, "Ignore it! Crowd it out! Do whatever you have to! But it goes back where it came from! We can study it later!"

"But S—"

"DO IT!! Remember your training!! Mirror and Conceal! That's an order!!"

So they did. The babbling Interfacer of his yesteryear had long since been trained and tested, and with a few expertly delivered distractions, it was all over. His Citizens went back to their games and their jobs, and business resumed as usual. And with neither wisdom nor humor, his Interfacers yelled to Bobby what they'd learned, saying, "I'm so sorry Bobby. I'm so sorry for your loss."

This was the way of the Sentient Cities. Burdened by a quandary so terrible, that it must be neither asked too loudly nor answered too well. So they didn't, and neither did Mann. Yet provision was never far away.

From the earliest accident of his youth, to the wrinkled cracks in his outer walls that seemed to grow every day, wear and tear were there.

Grinding facade and foundation, Citizen and stone, in their quest to make all Citykind listen to their proclamation; Either death's purpose is one of beginning, or life's purpose is meaningless end. Either life's purpose is more than is conceivable, or we are but a transient form of food to be soon forgotten, but for the plants and the soil and the worms.

A Note on Character

Well that took quite a turn, didn't it! So dark. So grim. Why do such a thing? It was going so well. Why ruin it with a thing like that?

Because this is how it was for the City of Mann. This is his story, not yours. You may have made your peace, and for that I commend you. But he had not. Even the thought of 'The Question' made him shudder. All by chance and all for nothing? Or all by design and for the purpose of another?! What a choice! His proverbial knees knocked at the implications. So choosing the illustrious third option,**18** he chose instead not to look, and hid it away.

But it's not what you're thinking. He was happier that way. Only forty years after starting his internship at CitiCorp he got his

---

18   **The Glorious Third Option**
            By Craddok Sturgeon (ISBN 43-08-12)

Shown the choice of A or B,
I grinned and picked the option three.
Asked to choose from 1 or 2,
I laughed and picked the number few.
Called to side with day or night,
I grabbed a blade and took my sight.
But sat in darkness on the floor,
I gasped; as there was choice no more.

first promotion, and only a short thirty seven years later that he became the office manager.

It was not just at work he succeeded either. Progress there came with progress everywhere else too. He was respected—liked even. Sought after for his expertise on one day and invited for drinks on the next.

'L'affluent Effluent' was one of his favorite places to go. A mix of artisanal wines and smooth jazz, it was the perfect antidote to the likes of 'Randy River's Brandy' or 'The Liquor Lagoon' that seemed to plague Epicurea's downtown. Catering to a more collected clientele, if rich fermented liquids and refined conversation were to your tastes, it was second to none.

Central Parklands was another place he liked to spend his time. Before moving away from it all, he had never even known that the sweet sound of silence or the softness of the grass under your hovernodes was something to be missed. But now, he knew it all too well. It was not far from his apartment lot, and he loved it there. Including his morning hovers, it was a rare day that he wouldn't visit, often meeting friends after work for a game of Bodgerobbit or even just to chat. On weekends in the summers, if he was lucky, he got to do both. Starting at the park at noon, it would be only till the sun was going down that he and his closest friends would head to L'affluent's. There, usually meeting up with others on the way, they would party into the night and all the struggle of the week before would be worth it.

As the Ruler of his City, Mann was quite tickled by the effect that other Cities had on his Citizens. Previously, if you recall, we talked about how the Citizens of each City made collective decisions. Well when a Citizen communicated a collective thought or idea with another, they would, like adding a drop of flavor to a recipe, impart a flavor of their personal thoughts and opinions with each other too. To this effect, all the different types of Citizen with their individual wants, can'ts, won'ts, likes and dislikes had a say in the overall decision making of the entire group; You remember, yes?

Well, this 'flavoring' of sorts, also worked in reverse. Just like how a Citizen added their own flavor to each idea before passing it along, sometimes the idea itself became like a flavor to them. Sometimes they found a thought or idea so interesting or peculiar that it stuck with them and in essence, they themselves, became 'flavored'. And when it did, it caused them to change.

In this way a Citizen would learn how to dance or discover what humor was. For example, on hearing a joke and finding it funny, a Citizen would nod it onto the next Citizen, flavored with laughter. Then they might say to themselves, 'I rather liked that very much. What was that?'

See how it stuck? Several iterations of humorous communications later, they would have a better understanding of what it was that made it funny, and several more again, they may even know enough to add to the joke themselves, making it even funnier!

However, it was not without its drawbacks. You see, in the same way a positive thing could be of intrigue, so could a negative thing. For as splendid as a note of humor can make something, a note of mockery or distrust can be destructive. So as Mann watched the destructive notes of Citykind flavor his little people, he began to grow concerned.

'But is this adaptation not simply the natural evolution of thought?' you mumble to yourself. 'How can a sentient consciousness be expected to survive if it does not build on its cumulative experience? Surely if they retained nothing, they would learn nothing?'

You are absolutely right, they would learn nothing. In fact, if it was not for this phenomenon, no City in the history of the planet would have ever progressed past the infant stage. Even the animals learned to some degree, and most of them were not very smart at all. So why then, the concern?

It was not the learning of his Citizens that concerned Mann, or even the type of 'flavor' that they learned. It was something else.

Long before he had agreed with his Politicians to move his City to Epicurea, he had noticed something curious about his Citizens. Outwardly, when things were going well, they were mostly nice and lovely. With their friends and amongst the collective, their behavior was largely for the good of others, striving for the betterment of the group and the City. Yet inwardly, it was not the same. Left alone in their funny little homes in their funny little bodies where no-one could see them, they were different. But Mann could see them. He could see them perfectly well. And what he saw was unusual.

When I said earlier that new thoughts and ideas kind of 'stuck' with a Citizen, I implied that it was almost by accident. But it was not. Actually, the more Mann watched his most precious Citizens, the more he saw how particular they were about what they retained. For as much as they appeared carefree and nonchalant, he saw that they never did anything without reason—never. And that reason was always the same one—themselves.

On the surface you would hardly be able to tell. He was not even convinced they were even aware of what motivated them, and if they were, it was so ingrained in their nature that they looked the other way. But it was always the same. Always with a motive and always with an angle. Every time. And every time, it was always for their own gain and profit. Each and every one of them, doing nothing for nothing. Not for the collective, or the City, or even their closest friends, unless it could be for the benefit of themselves.

"I will learn a joke to make someone laugh," they would say. 'Because then I will be seen as funny.'

"I will do a kind thing!" they would think. 'And forever be known as good!'

Even those who gave in silent anonymity sought the same prize. And when all was finished they would admire a deed well done, satisfied that the praise of others has less value than their own.

This bothered Mann a great deal.

"This couldn't be right," he had thought to himself. "But maybe it makes sense. After all, they are only simple creatures made to survive. And how can they be expected to survive if they do not think of themselves? Anyway, they can't all be like this, there must be some exceptions? My people are kind and good and loving at heart, not completely self centered! And sure, some are worse than others, they're not perfect—but there must be some mistake. Come on, look at them! Look how nice they are! They mean well, and they're doing their best. Besides, in so many ways they are me! We are one and the same. The sum of all our parts we are the City of Mann! Why, if they truly did nothing for anyone but themselves it would be as good as saying that I did nothing for anyone but myself! And that is simply not true! I have been the arbitrator and decider for us all. When Friend City of Derek needed to be hovered home the other night it was I who arranged his fare. When my Co-worker City was late for work, it was I who covered for them. And the week before, when that most odious City of ill repute asked for a handout, I did not have to—and certainly took a risk—but yet I gave. They may be faulted and may make mistakes, but my beloved Citizens are certainly not incapable of doing good!"

So dismissing the notion as illogical, and to be Frank[19]— offended by it—he left well alone. Yet, it was a flavor he could never shake off, as if he himself had been tainted by its bitter taste.

19.
'The notion that all Sentient Cities are inherently selfish is not only preposterous, but a gross offense to the countless good works done by so many throughout the ages.'

– Delacourt, Francis. (1939) the Marvel of Citykind's Achievements. 3rd Edn. Thinkytown Books.

Chapter 7

BUSINESS AS USUAL

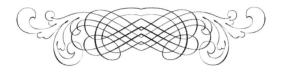

We previously discussed where infant Cities came from, and the ins and outs of the docking process at a City's South Gate. (Yes, you tittered like a schoolgirl then too!) So what about the other three gates?

"Trading resources!" you exclaim, having paid close attention to the chapter that came after. "And commodities!"

Yes, excellent! You are absolutely right. And I must say how happy I am to have someone so keen reading my words.[20] I can't tell you how demoralizing it can be as a writer to spend weeks and

---

20. On the basis of my work never being published on the planet of the Sentient Cities, I have made the assumption that you are a human being, reading human words on some kind of human sized apparatus, and not a Sentient City peeping down the Interfacer piece of a microscope at an interplanetary document written in a language you don't understand.

If I am wrong in this assumption I do apologize and congratulations on such a find.

months deliberating over every tiny detale, only to have a reader who is not bothered to pay attention.

"Aha!" you say, noticing that I wrote the last little bit to allow for those who did not remember to catch up. "You wrote the last little bit to allow for those who did not remember to catch up!"

Right you are again my friend, and bravo.

Trading was an absolute necessity for the Sentient Cities and as long as two of them were physically close enough, the trade of goods would occur. It didn't matter what two either—any two would do. Much as you might smell someone's perfume or hear their voice as you walk past them in a supermarket, to them, trading was merely a thing that happened; a facet of proximity and a fact of life. Of course the more time one spent with another the more trading would occur, but whether it was a brush with a stranger, or even an enemy, a trade between the two would invariably be made.

This peculiar exchange was possible because of one of the curious ways that they were made. It may be a little hard to picture, but a Sentient City hovering about their business— forwards and backwards and so on—did not do so while perfectly still. Instead, as their bulky mass moved in a particular direction, it did so in a continual rotation. Circular in shape, with its circumference equally covered by Interfacers, it made absolutely no difference which way they faced. So around and around they went. And using this unusual spinning movement to their advantage, they would trade.

Imagine, if you would, two Cities hovering in opposite directions down a street towards one another are preparing to pass. Both, as is their natural movement, are spinning at a steady rate. Neither knows the other, and once they have passed by and continued on their merry way, they will likely never see each other again.

Meanwhile, within their respective City walls, their relevant logistics departments have a full inventory of their City's resources and commodities. Priced already, surplus goods have been sent to the Traders in bulk and the list of their City's resource and commodity deficits has been issued. So as the gap between them dwindles, they wait.

Almost side by side now, the ground rumbles as the two massive Cities begin their pass and their gates rotate into position. This time the alignment is going to be North gate to West gate[21] alignment, and as they meet it is time for trading to begin.

Traders

Butted up against each of the three trading gates are the market districts. Aptly named North Market, East Market and West Market, every item that was not directly produced by a City itself could be purchased there. It was there that the Traders lived.

---

21. As it is inevitable that a City's South Gate will at some point accidentally align with another's gate, that is, a South to North, East, or West alignment, or even a (yikes!) South to South gate alignment, it is indeed very proper that the following etiquette be adhered to during trading rotations:
  - All Cities should keep their South Gates closed and locked at all times.
  - Where accidental alignment with a South gate occurs, all workers and traders posted at North, East or West should implement a position of 'distracted nonchalance.' (e.g. staring absentmindedly at clouds, whistling to oneself, examining fingernails, checking the time, etc.)

Citizens by any other name, their job was to balance their City's surplus and deficit goods. Too much granite after an over enthusiastic binge on mountain goats? No worries. Building materials needed for a new high-rise or a specialized part for the power plant? No problem. The traders could find it.

Rare items too. In fact, the rarer the better. If anything could be said about them, it was that they loved a good challenge. They took great pride in it, and, if they could make a little profit, no harm done.

Most of their days were spent either taking orders or selling stock in the markets, but it was the sound of the horns at the gate that was their call to action. Only signaling one thing, it was the most triumphant news that a Trader could hear; the news that an intercity gate alignment was about to occur. So shrieking with joy and excitement, they would abandon their shops and stands, and flood towards the City gate. Passing through it to the network of platforms and boardwalks that projected from the face of the City wall, they would gather in droves and wait, until, as the looming gate of the other City approached in rotation with its very own projecting platforms and very own Traders, they would prepare their dockets and clear their throats.

Watching a City pass another from afar, you might be puzzled by the timing of all of this. To your eyes, when a Sentient City passes another, they are really only side by side for a few short seconds and lined up gate to gate for even less. So how does it work? Surely there is not enough time for any trading to happen? A passing like this is barely enough time to say hello. But that is because you experience the passage of time quite differently than the Citizens of a City.

Nobody really knows why, maybe because of their comparative size or humorously short lives, but to them, a few short seconds in your time is closer to two or three hours in theirs. Even in the time it has taken you to read this sentence, the Traders would have already made their deals, shaken hands, loaded, craned and received all of the goods they planned to, counted them, and gone home. By the time you have gone to bed, a whole month for them has come and gone, and in it, many countless chances to trade.

The benefit of this, of course, was obvious. As a species, the Sentient Cities would never advance if they were bogged down by the minutiae of every trading interaction, but if the Traders did not have time to trade, nothing would get done. So this time difference was crucial. The side effect however, was that to a City as a collective, unified in thought and in structure—aware of the presence of its parts but symbiotically bound as a unit—trades seemed to happen almost instantaneously. This gave them very little oversight and regulation on what was imported. Outside items and influences would infiltrate their walls without their knowledge. And circulating among their Citizens long before they had even noticed, they were often left with the strangest feeling that within their own person they were not fully in control.

Imports

While a substantial portion of a Trader's time was spent importing raw goods and materials to build and maintain the City's infrastructure, they also catered to the whims of the individual Citizens. This was a good thing. Ruler Mann loved his Citizens and took great pride and enjoyment in watching them learn and grow. Even if he didn't, his purpose was to lead, not enslave. What benefit would his City gain from stifling the interests or talents of the people that populated it? So freely allowing them to import the things that they wanted, for the most part, was for gain.

He didn't have to go far to see their imports either. They couldn't seem to help themselves. Every one of their tiny houses brimmed with the latest appliance and shiniest technological device, and all were adorned with their personal flair. Art from Ville de Pompeux, shelves and cabinets from the Cities in the Northern Malms, and stacks of interesting but ultimately unsellable books by little known authors. No two Citizens were the same and the variety of their allure seemed to be endless.

He was not naive to their simple nature though. He had seen the dark side of some imports and the dire consequence they had on their owners. It wasn't like they wanted to do themselves harm, it just ended up like that sometimes. Do you think fanaticism starts as a fever, or obsession as a drug? Of course not. It usually starts with a single pleasant drop. An object of interest; a want, an idea, or a dislike, brought into their home through the front door. But whatever it was—they liked it. So they would look for more.

It did not have to be exactly the same, similar would do. And as their first became their second, and their second, their hundredth—each was consumed with more vigor than the last. Over time, slowly flavored by the object of their attention, many would not see the harm it was doing. Yet harm was done. Intoxicated by its aroma, their palate dulled and their words infused with its scent and when they nodded with the other Citizens, it was through a haze in which they saw and a fog through which they spoke. Driven and hungry to gorge on more of what they craved. The Collective, to them, becoming a mere means to grow and import more of their desire.

Mann had seen it and did not like it one bit. It could be horrible. Ask any of his Citizens about the Dissonance of 18979 incident, or the Fire of Ideation in the power plants. What his precious people could do to themselves was a horror. The scariest part was that it would happen outside of his control. He hardly ever saw it coming. There could be something in his City right now causing his people harm, and yet he wouldn't know! How ironic it was that the very people he chose not to enslave could give themselves as slaves to something else.

The Feign

You might be happy to know that not all of the woes of the City's Citizen were self-inflicted. Although self centered and definitely not free from making mistakes, they did not knowingly choose to harm themselves. But the Sentient Cities had an enemy.

Invisible but for the faintest shadow, they were known as the Feign. Naughty, nasty, tricky creatures, they were everywhere. Searching for a host on every shore and in every valley, they roamed the planet of the Sentient cities like whispered breaths of frigid wind.

When they found one, it was almost too easy. A City wouldn't even notice as they slipped over the wall or through a gate. And once inside, drifting through the streets with its Citizens, it would be time for them to play their games. . . . .

Oh, look, there! A car crash in the entertainment district is the perfect opportunity. A sanitation worker on his way home has misjudged the turn and rear-ended another.

'This will do nicely,' the Feign would whisper in their strange tongue. 'Look how angry he is!'

The anger is palpable. Not of the sanitation worker—he is still in his car with a badly injured leg. It's the other one, the businessman, whose expensive looking car has been hit. His car is ruined!

"What a stupid mistake," he yells. "Where did you learn to drive?! You'll be hearing from my lawyer!!"

'Delightful!!' the Feign giggle to each other in a gleeful hiss. 'Split up friendsss! You know what to do!'

Working their naughty magic, they set to task.

'Not just a ruined carrr,' they purr in the businessman's ear later that day. 'You missed your meeting because of that foooool.'

"I did, didn't I," the businessman grumbles. "I could have sworn I saw him on his phone. And now the merger has gone south. I should sue him!"

'Yessss! Sue him! Take him for all he is worth!'

"I'll crush him! I'll take him for all he is worth!"

'Yesssss, for all he's worth!!—And kill his doggggggg.'

"Yes! I'll kill his dog. . . . . . Wait, what?"

Don't worry, he didn't do that bit. The dog was just fine. But the sanitation worker was not. After the court case was over, his world was shaken. With a bad leg and in heavy debt to the bank, he was angry too. But he was different than the businessman. It was not his anger that was most useful to the Feign. It was his pride. With a whisper here and murmur there, it was not hard to push him deeper into his darker nature. With what little he had, he had worked so hard to build. He hadn't taken any handouts, or cut any corners. He had always done the honest thing. But now, here he was, injured and penniless—all because of some privileged Citizen's temper! And the judge had the nerve to say it was his fault! Where is the right in that?! Where is the justice?! It's just the rich siding with the rich, and the haves' with the have-mores'!

The more he listened, the more the Feign chattered. Research was a wonderful thing and alone by himself, he learned a great deal. That judge had sided with the gentry before! He was not alone in his injustice. There were others. Dozens like him—chewed up and swallowed by the very system they had given their lives to sustain—used and left to die.

Eventually, when he had healed and was due back to work, he declined. When his girlfriend tried to help, the Feign opened his eyes to her real motive. She enjoyed seeing him weak. She took pleasure in his helpless subservience! But he was better than her, better than them all!

'Yessss! You arrrre!'

So when the thought of making things right and taking a stand for all the downtrodden popped into his head; who better to do it than him?

After the incident, Ruler Mann was unsure of what to do. To calm his Citizens he told the newspapers that the bomber had acted alone. This was protocol. To his Citizens, the Feign were dismissed as folk tales and fantasy. But he and his Council knew the truth. They had seen the signs and read the report. It told clearly of the Feign. It told of the man's friends seeing their shadows and of a liquor store clerk who heard their voices. It stated the estimated type and number involved. The investigators had even traced them to a nearby family home. Yet, as all the times before, there was nothing that could be done. The Feign would not answer to the Citizens or Politicians—not even a Ruler! They wouldn't answer to anyone.

In the earlier years of his life, City of Mann had heard a wealth of who they were. But there was much disagreement. Some said they were devils,[22] wicked creatures from an unseen realm, while others refused to believe that they existed; a psychological trick of Citykind's imaginings disguised as an excuse to do wrong. Even so, despite their division, there was agreement on one thing. And that was the need to enforce the law.

---

22. " . . . . . . .of all the stars in the heavens, *he* was the brightest one! He was not a child! He did not need the Creator! He would create his own kingdoms, his own legions—him! His own life! An expanse of a new kind! An empire for his glory!!

So free to choose, Mahvett chose himself. But he was wrong. It was not life he could create. It was death. Darkness and abomination. For with his back to the light all he saw was shadow. So cast upon the planet, he and the Feign who followed him were banished. And there, as they hungered for Cities to devour, they lured the blind to his shining gloom."

- La Fossa del Re Sirena (The Pit of the Siren King) by Città di Romani, Vol. 1, pp. 18-32
ISBN 26-28-11/19

Chapter 8

LAW & ORDER

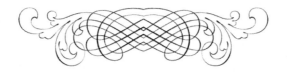

By itself, the law was not enough. Not long ago, if you recall, we talked about the Constitutional laws that were given to the Sentient Cities. And how, written on every wall and every street of every City, they were the foundational rules of which all law of every other type was derived. Well, there was a problem.

That bitter note of character that City of Mann had seen in himself was not exclusive to him. It was in all of them, seeking, searching and hungering only for the glory of themselves. Citykind had long argued about this too, with some calling it darkness, and others as 'survival by another name'. But instinct or nature, it did not matter. What mattered was the hell they knew it could bring. History had told that story quite well. And even with their myriad of rules and the law to end all laws written right in their core, it was only a matter of time before a City and its Citizens would come to harm another.

It would start only as a little want. A pretty thing. Control, or love, or money. Yet, though tame at first, want would nurture obsession. Citizens would bring it gifts and food, and soon, speaking its name and bowing to its glory, the streets would fill with dancing and music. Their fervent cheer raising clouds of dust and smoke, wine would fill their bellies and bliss would cloud their minds, until, as the words of the hallowed Constitution faded from their sight, they were freed from its decree. It is then that their hunger would pass into the real world. Hungry for more, more than it cared it caused harm the City would roam the planet inflicting its want on Citykind.

It took time for Mann to see it, but looking to the world and how it was ruled, he came to a conclusion. Within his City, the Constitution was not enough. Order had to be enforced. He loved his Citizens dearly, but they were too easily led and swayed. He could not change their hearts or their silly ways. What else was he to do? They were his responsibility and he was the Ruler. And now, with the Feign at play, they needed more—his City needed more.

Chapter 9

ALL HAIL MANN

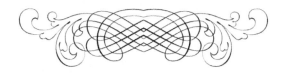

I t was hard at first. Tours of his City and endless meetings with the Politicians. Late nights and early mornings. New departments and leaders—battling and compromising to appease them all. Yet as drafts grew to final laws and he marked them with the final strokes of his pen, Ruler Mann's system of law and order came to be.

To the world outside his walls, his City had made it.

He, Senior Manager City of Mann (MA B.Soc.Sc DipTh) was a success. He had played the game and won. An exemplary model of the Great Sentient Citykind. A gracious boss and a humble friend. Revered as an associate and worthy as an adversary. Matchless under pressure and a joy to have on any team. Shrewd and calculated, kind and fair. An asset and a champion for whom everyone had respect. Yet this was the least of it. Inside his City, he was a God. The Great Ruler Mann—Lord of the Great City of Mann! He was so very proud. His Citizens adored him. His intellect was unparalleled! All questions to him, all answers from him! The rock of reason and the arbiter of truth!

THE CITY FALLS
INTO CHAOS

W ell, my friend. You have learned much indeed. You have seen how, with stone set on stone, our Cities are formed. You have seen the sweeping parapets of our walls and the towering pinnacles of our facades. You have seen the construction of thought into word and how, dotted with footnotes[23] and titles, word transforms into meaning. You have seen the inner workings of our minds and our feelings, and how, free to choose, we are bound by the limits of our freedom.

So then, having your own knowledge of reality itself and knowing the foundation on which the Sentient Cities stand, you know well of the cracks, and what will happen next.

23.

'Soliloquy of a Sidenote'
From 'The Book Who Found its Voice' (page 53, footnote 21)
by N. Owen (ISBN 54-01-12/17)

I am dirt. I am dust. I am nothing. A shadow of what I hope.
I am ash, faded chalk. I am absent. A fragrant wisp of smoke.
Lowest of the low. I am the weakest of the weak.
I am mouth of knives and tongue of broken glass when I speak.
I am shaking hands, I am stifled breath.
I am a wounded doe, who pants in longing for her death.
Yet as I have hope, I have been given.
All is purpose. All is provision.
For if I am mute, I'll have quiet to think.
If I am a footnote, I will sing to you in pen and ink.
If I am but a sound, in a song to you I speak.
And if I am dirt I'll lift you higher, from low beneath your feet.

Chapter 10

ANARCHY

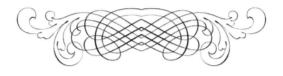

When exactly it started, Ruler Mann did not know. He suspected it must have happened long before he had even noticed the first little change. Perhaps longer still before that. His City and his most precious Citizens were always his priority, and the flashes of it he was seeing now were much too audacious to be new. The dribs of and drabs of disquiet must have first surfaced elsewhere, beyond where he often looked. A home maybe. The dissatisfaction of a mother or a father. Or a restless boredom turned contempt by their adult kids. Who knew? But 'why' was a better question. What was it that they lacked?

Mann had dedicated his life to his Citizens, given them everything and coddled them since their collective birth. When they had struggled with their first mud huts, it was he who told them how to build. It was he who taught them to speak and to trade and he who comforted their fears! When they needed respite he gave them calm, and when they needed order he wrote their laws. What more did they want? He had given them everything. He allowed the rise of their Politicians and listened to all their often foolish words. Even when they demanded more power—his power—he compromised and showed them mercy. By his will they had advanced and flourished, and by his will they had prospered. Everything they were as a Sentient City amongst the gentrified of Epicurea was because of him!

But it hardly mattered. For whatever reason, it was as clear as day; it was not enough. His people longed for more. Dissension was boiling. Corruption and scandal seemed to ooze from their homes and halls. Crime was rising in ways he had never seen before. And grievance toward themselves, each other and even Mann himself hissed beneath their skin like venomous snakes.

Idols

Mann's Citizens had always liked the things that they liked. Who doesn't. Music, dance, reading, art, debate, alone-time, wine, swimming, long walks on the wall, comedy, company, the male form, the female form, more wine, hats, nature, giving, getting, morning, night, laughter, kindness, revenge, rain, kooky spectacles, and so on—there were so many things that they had likes for I could continue for a very long time. And although I am sure some of you paused to tut in disapproval at the more risqué enjoyments, I imagine you share at least some of these likes too. Yet, it was not any one object of enjoyment that was causing a major issue, or even a combination of them all. It was something else.

Named after Professor City of Adula, who first defined its existence, the BIA (City of Mann Bureau of Internal Affairs)[24] called it Adulation.

'An inherent facet of all Citizens of Citykind', she wrote in issue #261 of the Journal of Metropolic Neuroscience, 'Adulation is the manifestation of their psychological need to worship'.

How this fancy description translated in the real world was quite apparent. Drifting over the homes in the residential areas, Ruler Mann could see its effects. For some it was sports. A game to be watched, a team to be followed. A jersey to be worn and a bet to be placed. A match—the match. A win—our win! We won!! Goooal!!! Mann would laugh as they spilled popcorn and beer in their delight! His lovely little Citizens were so funny sometimes! For others who did not like the sports so much it could be fashion, politics, family or even their own faces—anything at all. But whatever it was, it only became a problem for the City when they raised it higher than it ought to be raised.

For Citizen Dorian Chaddick, it was The Society of Precocious Gentlemen. He just loved what it stood for and loved to debate. For Carla Stack it was her job. It challenged her and defined her, and made her who she was. Keith Maranthian was enthralled with his impressive collection of classic records. And yet, it was not the Adulations like these that Mann or the BIA were too concerned with. Not yet. It was what could happen next. Striving for the

---

24. Opened in 20948 as a direct response to the Christmas party event of the previous year and the subsequent workplace disciplinary action taken against City of Mann by CitiCorp (BIA event #001), the BIA was established to investigate threats to City security caused by fanatically ecstatic or despondent members or groups of the Collective Citizenship.

Located in the downtown entertainment district on the corner of Selfy Ave. and Awarington St. the City of Mann Bureau of Internal Affairs is open Monday-Friday, 9am to 5pm.

thing that they loved so much, soon they would do what all good Citizens do best—build!

In their living room to start, a small shrine to their desire would be stood. Then a carving for the kitchen, perhaps somewhere close to the sink. Building and building, trinkets and sculptures for the bedrooms would be next, and once the whole house was cluttered they would move outside to the garden.

"Come one, come all!" they would call in excitement, as they constructed another, this one a huge statue in gold. "Come and see this great thing that I have found! Look what it has done for me!!"

Spilling onto the streets, many would hear and come to see. And as they too became enamored at the shiny thing, the festivities would begin. Drums beating in a thunderous rhythm, acrobats and dancers would spin and frolic. Smoke billowing through the elated crowd, strobing lasers and luminous lighting would flicker and flash as they sang and screamed in jubilation. Wine would flow like water, and soon all thought other than the present time would be forgotten.

Among the Citizens of the City of Mann, or indeed those of any Sentient City, Adulation and its parties was not uncommon. Most ended by themselves. It nearly cost Carla her marriage before she left hers behind and Keith just got bored with his and moved on. But decades after the BIA had been alerted, Dorian Chaddick's had not stopped at all, his had spread and grown. Statues and symbols of The Society of Precocious Gentlemen were everywhere and their supporters were thousands strong. Everywhere you looked they had representatives. In union halls and boardrooms, working and deliberating to gently sow their aspirations.

They were not the only ones whose desires had grown to hold power either. A like of any kind with enough support could gain influence, and a means to influence was a dangerous thing. Mann knew this well. As way back when his City was in its infancy, long before The Society of Precocious Gentlemen or even the BIA, he had first seen its true power.

It was springtime when it happened. Other than to celebrate him, their Great Spirit Ruler, it was the largest gathering of Citizens he had ever seen. All that morning, reports had been coming into the Temple. At the beginning it was only of traffic disruptions in the Industrial district. But when he heard that his own people were hurting each other and then that a lawkeeper had been injured, he was deeply troubled. So taking to the sky, he flew east to soothe his ailing kin. Spotting a cloud of smoke rising over several factories, the distant din of music grew loud as he dove towards them. And as the form of a great statue came into view, he realized what they were all there for.

An object of fascination that had come into the City months ago, it was known as Chocolate. A substance, he was told,**25** with a special kind of more-ishness. Sweet, yet delightfully rich and creamy. He had thought nothing of it at the time. His Citizens seemed to like it, so what more was there to it? All he wanted was for them to be happy.

But this. . . This was not what he had expected would come of it. Thousands upon thousands of his beautiful people, wildly thrashing in mirth and merriment in reverent worship of. . . what was this? This was not how it was supposed to be! Were they unaware of the harm they were doing? Fires raged around them from petrol bombs they had thrown. Unbelievers were dragged to their knees and forced to convert. Sirens wailed as paramedics and lawkeepers helped who they could. And all as they sang and bowed to the magnificent golden figure of the sweet snack that towered above.

"Stop, my children!" Mann had yelled at his beloved Citizens. "Stop!!"

They did not stop. Their numbers surging, the crowds moved down the street whooping in delight and laughter. More mayhem. More violence. The music grew louder. Was it that they could not hear him?

"Citizens of Mann!!" he screamed, "I said STOPPP!!"

Bellowing with a maelstrom of fury, he unleashed the power of his voice, blasting the roofs of several adjacent buildings to pieces and sending hoards of revelers scattering to the ground.

For a moment there was an eerie silence, as scrambling to their feet they looked upward to where the mighty force of his authority had come from. But then, with a shrug, they looked to one another and began to nod. And one after another, as they synchronized in their common desire to return to their statue, they turned and faced the other way.

25.

Excerpt from 'Rejection of a Mother's Love', by Spirit Ruler Clara to the Citizens of Nurse City of Clara

'. . . . . Incompatible with the nourishment of my Citizens realm, a being such as I still wonders of the tastes and smells that allure my people so. And I mourn. But not for myself. For by what I am sustained is so much more and it is them who do not know of its provision. For the realm that I belong is unseen to them, and unheard. Of its sweet fragrance they know little—of its honeyed tone they know less. It is they who have smelled not and they who have tasted not. Blind to all I wish to give, and short of all I wish them to receive, they neither see my face nor hear my voice or feel the touch of my warm embrace. Yet, I will persevere. As I am theirs. And they are my beloved.'

Mann reeled in confusion. What was this madness? Did they just turn their backs on him?! Yet as the drums and music returned to life he watched aghast as they resumed their march.

Reaching the edge of the residential district, they continued their rampage, proclaiming the chocolatey goodness, converting as many as they found and killing all who resisted.

"Please, little ones!" Mann pleaded. "Stop!! Can't you see what you're doing to yourselves?!! This is not who you were meant to be!!!"

Desperately pulling some to safety he pushed swathes of others back. But their numbers were too great. No matter how many he held back or how many fires he extinguished, their destruction spread.

Their harmonious nodding was spreading too. With each collective question or query that came and went from the greater Citizens' Collective, they shared the single focus of their newfound love.

'You must try it,' they communed. 'It will change you and complete you! You will be a better you! We will be a better us!! We must have more, we can have more! We can have it all!'

How it ended was well documented by several news outlets, as well as being given prominence by the indie docu-series, 'Mad for Chocolate', released the following year. As incidents popped up all over the City, the Adulationists eventually took control of one of the City control centers and hijacked a component of Interfacer command. All while City of Mann, only a youngster at the time, was in the aisles of a grocery store with his Parent City.

The results were disastrous. What had started as a request for a sweet treat, turned quickly into a rage, and demanding not just some, but all of the chocolate, he flew into a tantrum.

According to witness, City of Phoebe, who was the store clerk at the time:

"I was packing freezers when I saw him first, just after my break. And I was shocked. I've never heard an infant City talk to its Parent like that! I mean. . . the things he said! I didn't know what to do, so I went to go and get help. I guess I must have spilled some of the frozen livestock mini's on the floor. As next thing I know, this older gentleman—one of our regular Customer Cities—slips on it and comes crashing through the shelves of aisle eleven. You probably don't know the shop layout, but eleven is nothing but snacks and treats, and all of a sudden—it was like the little fella could smell it—he went berserk! Breaking away from his Parent he charged past me and started vacuum tubing everything! And when the Security Cities got to where he was kind of hunched sideways on the pile of food—he just growled at them like a demented bird. Took three of them to get him off it!"

It was in that moment that Ruler Mann had realized his weakness. His darling Citizens, his beautiful people, they did not live to serve him. They were not bound to listen to his voice or obey his words. With whatever power he had, it would never be enough. Even if it would lead them to death and ruin, tossed to and fro by whim or fancy, they would serve only what they believed would serve them.

Politicians

I suppose it is silly of me to have gotten this far without talking a little more about the Politicians.

For as much as the Citizens hungered for their desires, they had a requirement for their needs. What good, after all, was the fulfillment of a secondary urge, without the satiation of the higher things that sustained them first? There were mouths to feed and homes to be built. Courts to protect their interests and lawkeepers to patrol their streets. Jobs to be secured and the safety of resilient economic planning. Even then, safe and fed and clothed, they had a need to be loved and belong. And finally, if being able to contribute and partake, they may finally be content—for a while at least. For they too had a need to be satisfied in themselves and have mental and emotional fulfillment.

As this was no small task, Mann knew it was impossible to provide for them all by himself. By his one hundredth birthday, his population was already nine hundred thousand and by the end of his second year in Junior school it had reached two million. With so many Citizens and so many needs, a Ruling Spirit of any ability would have been stretched thin, let alone him, so the appointment of Citizens to speak on their behalf was the logical thing to do. With needs categorized and combined, a hierarchy was established, and the ruling structure of his magnificent City was formed. And at his right hand, the ones who the Citizens had chosen, were called the Politicians.

There were far more than I have time to tell so I will not name them all. But there are a few names that are good to know.

Counter of things, numerator and tallier of all things real and imaginary, living & dead, was King Quantis of Currencia. All needs related to fairness and equality were addressed by him. Food and finance. How one was treated by another or how one compared to someone else. King Quantis quantified every aspect of the City and its people, weighing its worth and value with impeccable measure. Then there was his most Wise & Exceptional Grace, the Humble High Priest of Pride.**26**

Second daughter to the King of Peek & Envylia, there was Lady Wanting of the Wandering Eye. She vied for every Citizen's right to have at least as much as their neighbors.

Lord Pahnik the Fourth was the fourth in his line who spoke for the fearful and anxious. He was known for his shrill and quavering voice. And fighting for the Citizens' right to satisfaction and ease was the Silken Queen of Sufficience, from Contentment's plush and rolling hills.

---

26. "Order! Order!!" the Council Head yelled over the shouts of the Politicians, banging his mallet on the podium in frustration. "This is an assembly meeting, not a schoolhouse! Order!!"

As the red faced Politicians returned to their seats, Ruler Mann rolled his eyes at the spectacle, and shuffled in his throne.

"Good," the Council Head continued, as silence returned. "Now, the agenda for the—"

With a loud creak, the huge doors of the council chambers swung open. All heads turning to the sound, a man entered. Impeccably dressed in furred robes—a cleric or priest of some sort—he was adorned in jewels and gems and had a neat golden crown.

"Can we help you?" the Council Head addressed him.

"Yes, yes," the man muttered to himself as he cast a contemplative gaze around the room. "This will do." With a clip in his step he began to march across the concourse.

"Excuse me, sir. You can't be in here. Sir! This is a private assembly of elected council members only!!"

Indifferent to the protestations, the man continued on his way as the host of Politicians watched on in quiet disbelief. And then, grabbing an empty chair at the far side, he dragged it screeching behind him across the floor and up the steps of the royal platform.

"Sir! I will not ask you again!!" the Council Head roared. "Someone call security!!"

Stopping beside the throne of a most perplexed Ruler Mann the man shimmied his chair into position. And sitting down with a deep and satisfied breath, he muttered "Yes, this will do nicely, indeed."

– Taken from Melville Taft's; **Diary of a Courtroom Clerk,**
Chapter 3: The Priest of Pride Resides (ISBN 19-10-04)

Striving for the will of the people, there were many more too, one to suit every flavor. But what mattered was that it worked. For as much as Mann despised the Temple Assembly where they argued about what was right for the people, he could not imagine his world any other way. Yet, there was a catch.

It was only a matter of days from their election that Statues of them could be seen everywhere. Cast in bronze and adorned in gold and silver, huge monoliths of familiar forms that he knew well. Adulation, you see, did not discriminate on the object of its affection and the Politicians promised to give many things indeed. Mann was concerned by this at first, but after much discussion with the BIA he allowed it. As long as the Citizens' newfound object of worship didn't threaten the City as a whole, what difference did it make? He was not blind to their tricks or their hunger for power, but it was a small price to pay for their support.

Crime and Punishment

Standing before the tall windows of the great hall that overlooked his City, Ruler Mann took a deep breath and sighed.

Truth be told, although his people had done so for many years, he was still saddened to see them bow down to the forms of others. Yet, for whatever pain it caused him, nothing compared to the pain of watching them turn on each other.

Another rising column of smoke in the distance caught his attention—somewhere out in the industrial district by the look of it.

'What now?' he thought to himself.

It was only the previous week that the violence in that district had flared up again, and only the week before that he'd sent the BIA to subdue yet another group of Adulationists in Safengshire.

He loved his people, he really did, but as the years of his life went on, it began to seem that there was nothing they were incapable of. His City and what it had become was such a place of contradiction! I mean, it was undoubtably a modern marvel of technological accomplishment and design. But for all the knowledge and power it had given to its inhabitants—of real wisdom and virtue they seemed to have gained nothing at all.

"Lord Mann! Lord Mann!!" the nasal sound of Gibald, his new steward, echoed through the silence of the hall. "Are you here?!"

"Yes boy. I am here," Mann replied. "What is it?"

Rushing past him to the empty throne, the lad dropped to his knees before the vacant seat and bowed his head.

"My Lord. Forgive my intrusion. Commander Strive sent me to request your presence."

Mann paused for a moment, watching the young fellow from behind, slightly unsure of what to do without startling him. "Don't be alar—"

"Eeeek!!" Gibald shrieked, clambering to his feet to gawk around the room in frantic confusion. "Sire! My apologies! I didn't know! I thought you were—"

"It's alright, It's alright," Mann soothed him. "No need to fret. I'm over here, by the window. See my shadow, yes? Good. And no apologies. You'll get used to it. The acoustics in this place are not conducive to easy interaction. Tell me—what has happened?"

"Yes, of course. Thank you my Lord," Gibald added, rather shaken by the encounter. "I'm afraid there has been another riot. A few, actually. Two in Worthington and one in Bodingsley. The Commander has called a meeting in the Situation Room."

Typical for this time of day, the Temple was busy. The Politicians wheeled and dealed in their chambers, while traders sold goods of every kind in the corridors and halls. When it had become like this, Mann did not fully know. But seeing them pushing and shoving in what was supposed to be a place of reverence and peace, only added to his growing frustration. His precious Citizens were once so easy to please—in the days of his youth, when all they had were mud huts and straw roofs. Back then, there was not much that could not be solved by a warm meal and a merry sing-song. But now they found the things that had once enamored them dull and gray. They seemed so tired and restless. Rarely content or grateful—never still. Always in search for the next thing. Abundant in everything but satisfied with nothing.

Clearing his throat as he entered, the men and women of BIA command fell silent as he drifted through the wall. "Good morning Citizens," he said.

"Lord Mann," Commander Strive greeted him. "Thank you for coming on such short notice."

"Don't mind that," Mann responded, taking his seat at the head of the long table. "What has happened this time? I assume it is not good news."

"No my Lord, I am afraid not. There has been another spate of riots across the districts. Two in—"

"Yes Commander," he interrupted, "I know—Worthington and Bodingsley—what is new? Did you break me away from my narrative musings to tell me that?"

"No my Lord. It is not just that. The riots in Worthington and Bodingsley were late last night. There have been eight more this morning, some from as far out as Safenshire and Belonginham."

"Eight? Just this morning? Are you sure?!"

"Yes Sire. And there's more. We have just received news of one in Purposet."

"Purposet!" Mann exclaimed. "Not Purposet![27] Good Lord! Whatever will we do?"

"Yes my Lord, we were hoping you would tell us too. The Lawkeepers are overrun. We have mobilized the BIA troops, but the rate things are spreading we are looking at a Citywide emergency by dinnertime. If that happens it is only a matter of time before someone takes control of the City's functions."

Mann was alarmed. A loss of the City's functions to the fanatics never ended well. Drawing a deep breath, he looked around at his pale faced staff as they expectantly looked back, "Who is responsible for it this time? Do we know?"

---

27. Of all the districts that there were, Purposet was by far the loveliest. Unlike Citizens from the other districts—like the cretins in Bodingsley who were mostly concerned with their physical needs, or the affectionate and loving simpletons of Belonginham, Purposites did not waste their days worrying about their basic requirements, but rather thinking about their higher calling. In robes of purples and scarlet, they were the philosophers, the dreamers, and the entrepreneurs. The great thinkers, who, in their glittered district of mirrored glass and Elysian mist, studied and mused their City's greater purpose in the world.

"There seems to be several groups, my Lord. The Silken Queen's followers and the Golden Calfers.**28** The Watchers of the Mirror from Bodingsley and the CitiCorp Veneraters from Worthington as well. There's a new group too, down in the entertainment sector, worshiping a statue of a City with a remarkably curvaceous undercarriage. We don't know much about them yet, but their followers seem to be popping up all over the City. There are others too, reports are coming in faster than we can handle them. And Feign activity is up threefold since last week. I have given the order for BIA spectral division to deploy the FeignFlayer2000 as we speak, but they are cautious after last time." **29**

The room fell quiet as Mann pontificated the news. "This is not good," he said after some time. "Not good at all."

"No my Lord, it is not."

"And the Politicians? What do they have to say?"

"The Politicians Sire?"

"Yes Commander! The Politicians! What are they doing?"

28.
One of the more puzzling groups of Adulationists that ever rose to proliferation in the City were the Golden Calfers. Quite taken with baby cows for one reason or another, they were originally heralded as 'friends of the earth' by CETA and the SPCA. But after much vandalism, looting, destruction of property, kidnapping and murder, rumors spread that this was potentially untrue. This led to a rise in Citizen-Bovine tensions that had been unseen for decades, with cows being blamed for many types of ailment and calamity.

Despite increasing pressure from both the opposition and activists, Ruler Mann reiterated his stance that, *"No cow of any kind can, or will, be held accountable for any ill of any kind. The legal system will not be used to persecute these creatures—They are just cows!"*

"They are, working Sire—liaising—with the, em, local residents and such, you know, to find a diplomatic solution to end this terrible mess."

Mann bristled at the Commander's words. "Commander Strive! Are you looking to become a Politician yourself? Maybe you too could have your own statue and your own obedient Citizens? An army of little Strives working their little efforts for your glorious gain!"

"No my Lord, I—"

"Well don't spare me the truth then!"

"Of course my Lord. My apologies. I don't know how to say it. Honestly. . . they seem to be. . ."

---

29.   CITY BLOCK VAPORIZED BY SPECTRAL SNAFU

Local residents of downtown's Safenshire district were woken this morning by yet another of the long string of mishaps related to BIA's Spectral Division's long awaited, 'FeignFlayer'. Firing upon a suspected Feign hideout from a military helicopter, the energy weapon turned the 400 block of Kensington into ash, instantly vaporizing its inhabitants.

The nine thousand, nine hundredth and ninety ninth iteration of the controversial weapon, critics of its viability claim it has yet to have eliminated a single Feign. Advocates for its development, including Lord Pahnik IV, stand by their statement, that a little collateral damage is natural, and expect the FeignFlayer2000 that is to be released in Spring of next year to be a great improvement.

Names of the seven hundred and fifty two victims will be added to the memorial wall of the FeignFlayer memorial gardens during a service later this week.

—Structural Gazette. 276/27/20184

Mann's frustration had reached the end of its limits. "Seem to be what?!!?!!" he roared, sending paperwork on the table flying into the air and several of his staff tumbling backward off their seats. "Out with it!!!"

"They are making it worse, Sire!!" the Commander blurted out. "They're stirring it up! Justifying it!! Condoning it!!! Lady Wanting has sided with the Watchers and is negotiating with this new 'Curvy City' group to crush the grieving civilians in Worthington. She says the people of Bodington want what they want and will do anything to get it! King Quantis doesn't seem to care! He is taking bets on the winners and has invested big in the property market in the affected areas. The Silken Queen seems to be playing both sides and the High Priest has declared lordship over all of Worthington and is headed for Purposet! He's having his face etched onto the CitiCorp statues too—I don't know why, but it cannot be good! And Lord Pahnik!? That one was never right, but now he seems to have lost his mind! He is handing out weapons in the streets to anyone who will take one It's chaos, my Lord! Chaos!!"

Drawing a long breath, Mann raised his hand for silence, "That is enough Commander," he spoke with a tone of solemn surety. "Thank you—but please, I have heard enough. All of you... You are dismissed. I will take it from here."

Mann knew what he had to do. He had done it before. But his beloved people had not learned. They never learned! The glorious City of Mann was not born to be a creature of impulse—it was more than that! It was not some mere animal led by desire and ruled by emotion. It was one of the Great Sentient Cities—his Great Sentient City! And although they were its people, he was its king! Why would they not listen?! Why would they not change?!

Could they not see the harm they were doing to each other? To themselves?

It did not matter, they had given him no choice. If they wanted to bow so much he would bend their necks and if they wanted to kneel so badly he would sweep them off their legs!

Bursting out of the roof of the Temple, anger burned in his belly as he hurtled towards the black columns of smoke. He would make them listen. He would make them change! And as the sky roared with the sound of his rage, the ground shook as he descended on the first crowd of unruly Citizens.

Screams of terror filling the air, the streets ran red with blood as he began to lay waste to their ranks. Dashing them to pieces, he hammered and smashed and crushed everything in his fury, turning buildings to rubble and dust.

On arrival of the BIA troops, those who survived begged for mercy, howling with sorrow as they were rounded up and chained in lines. So at last, when the carnage of Mann's justice had come to an end, the City lay silent in awe of his brutal might. He had won. He had spoken. Yet, as he gazed upon the emptiness of his destruction, he couldn't help but feel it was a defeat.

Chapter 11

WAR

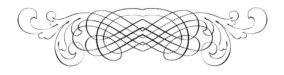

CitiCorp's Vice President, City of Caspian, was a rather unpleasant City. Or at least City of Mann thought so. A family friend of the company CEO, he had joined the company fifty nine years after City of Mann and after only a few short months, risen quickly up the managerial ladder. Setting a new record, he was the youngest of all the managers. Yet where he lacked in experience he made up for with his unbridled confidence, having the remarkable knack of putting all his failures down to anything but his own fault. City of Mann did not hold this against him. Not at the start at least.

In the beginning, they were friends. Taking the time to train him up on all the systems, it was Mann who had conducted his orientation and Mann who had invited him out with the work group for drinks. But over time something shifted. Mann had thought nothing of it at first, just a young City looking to make a name for himself. But when the team—Mann's team—was called for a meeting and Mann was nowhere to be seen, it was City of Caspian who had headed it up.

'I wouldn't worry about it,' he had been told when he expressed his displeasure. 'It was an accident. He wouldn't have done it on purpose.'

So not worrying, he put it out of his head. Till it happened again.

Not long after, on a day he was absent, a groundbreaking presentation on FAWP[30]—*His* groundbreaking presentation on FAWP—was given to the directors without any mention of his name!

A misunderstanding, Caspian claimed. He and Mann had talked it over before and he was only doing what he thought Mann wanted. But it was no accident. Mann had worked on it for months. It was *his* brainchild. The presentation was arranged to be done the following week by *him*—not Caspian! He had even put it in the team workflow. He put everything in the workflow! That's how Caspian knew he was with the facadeoligist that day for his biannual whitening. The scoundrel!

Yet beyond all the sleights and subtleties that increasingly gnawed away at Mann's patience, what bothered him the most, was that no one else seemed to notice. Some even thought Caspian was charming and dismissed the treacherous injustice he exuded as youthful enthusiasm. Even City of Susan from accounting seemed to be fooled by his wiles. So as a slow simmer of bitterness and resentment began to boil inside his walls, hateful thoughts turned to war.

---

30. (The **F**uture of **A**cronyms in the **W**ork **P**lace)

An Eye for an Eye

Ruler Mann had long heard of his Citizens' distaste for City of Caspian. Spoken of with malice by King Quantis and trembling contempt by Lord Pahnik, the utterance of his loathsome name grew in frequency within the Temple. When finally the position of Vice President went to him, leaving City of Mann subservient to his cocky ignorance, favor for diplomacy had worn thin.

"How do you call yourself a leader, Lord Mann?" the Humble High Priest scoffed during the Council Assembly. "Your weakness has made us all weak!!"

"Hear, hear!!" the Politicians concurred from the crowded chamber floor.

"Is our great City," he continued, "Our image, our status and our power—all that we are—to be subservient to this City of Caspian, a mere child!! Ha! Spirit 'Ruler' indeed! We know the Spirit-Mann, but where is this Ruler!?!"

"Yes! Hear, Hear!!"

"We the people demand answers Sir, what say you?"

Mann's anger burned in his head. Listening to their ungrateful taunts and jeers, he did not know who he hated more—them or that reprobate, City of Caspian.

Rising from his throne he cleared his throat. "Ladies and Gentlemen of the Council," he spoke. "I will remind you of who you all are and whose house you are in. It is by my hand that you sit in your positions of power, and by my will that you draw every breath. Do you question my authority?"

As the weight of his booming voice echoed to nothing, the chamber fell into silence.

"Good. Before I give you your answer, I will remind you too of the price we have paid for our actions. Classmate City of Eldridge?

BankClerk City of Julian? Girlfriend City of Deirdre?! Are these names you have forgotten? Coworker City of Peter, or maybe Dean City of Eleanor? These wars did not come free! They cost lives! Not just of our enemies, but ours—our Citizens. And our Citizens who are forever scarred—those who were damaged, corrupted and jaded by the things that they have done. So, for all my fault, I hope you know that my decisions for war or diplomacy have always been for you."

As a lone hiccup from a dreadfully embarrassed clerk resounded through the eerie hush, Mann inhaled deeply, pausing momentarily for dramatic effect.

"But. . ." he added, "The time for diplomacy is over." The Politicians and dignitaries standing to their feet in cheer, his voice rose in commanding fervor, "We have endured enough and we will take it no more!! And when we are finished, every Citizen of this City of Caspian will remember our name!! So today, I, Spirit Ruler Mann of the Great Sentient City of Mann, declare war!"

A Tooth for a Tooth

Roll out the weapons of war. Roll out the objects of intent. City of Mann is going to war! Sirens wailed as the news nodded across the City. The rattle of shop fronts and shutters slamming closed rang out. Parents rushed their children indoors. And as a stifled foreboding hung heavy in the stillness, a myriad of shrieks howled from the corners of the darkest streets, as the Feign smelled the desire of Mann's heart.

"Places everybody!" Gibald squeaked, as the rushing wind of Mann's arrival blustered down the corridor towards the Situation Room. "He's coming!"

The heavy doors closing behind him, Mann entered, frowning as he took his place at the head of the war council. Pausing to take a long look at his advisors and Politicians seated around the table, he began to speak.

"Commander Strive. Please, update us on our progress."

"Yes my Lord," the Commander replied. "We are ready and awaiting your orders. The Interfacers have been briefed and the Dreadapults are loaded."

"And the Typist?"

"Yes Sire. We have just heard back from the hall of records. He is ready and waiting for the Politicians."

"Good. Is everybody else ready? " Mann addressed the room.

"Yes my Lord," they responded in chorus.

"Good then, let us do what we must. High Priest, King Quantis—go to the typist and assist him with his fabrications. I want something shocking yet believable, something Caspian will not hesitate to believe. Play to his ego, it is a weak point we can exploit. And to anyone else that will listen, feed their sense of injustice. Most of them will need no more than a nudge— Caspian's age and arrogance is not to his favor. Lady Wanting, go with them too. Your expertise will be invaluable. And Silken Queen, I want you to the districts to distract the people with your comforts. Give them some help to look the other way. And Lord Pahnik. . ."

"Y-y-yes Sire?" Lord Pahnik jittered, wiping the perspiration from his brow with his sleeve.

"If we have panic in the streets now, we will fail. Can you keep it together until we are done?"

"Well, yes sir—I mean, Sire. I. . . I think. . . but shouldn't the people know the risks? Don't they have a right to fear?! What if it goes wrong? What if we get caught?! We could lose our friends—

our job!! And if we lose our job—what would we do for income?! We could lose our home!!!!!"

"Lord Pahnik!" Mann interrupted him as the throes of hyperventilation shrieked from his lungs. But it was too late.

"WE COULD LOSE EVERYTHING!!" he shrieked, "AGHHHHH!!!!!!!!!!!!!!!" Knocking his chair aside and scrambling frantically to his feet he clutched his hair in his hands before bolting for the door.

"Not again!" Mann yelled. "Guards! Follow him!! Keep him out of the City!—And bring him his paper bag!!"

The sounds of screaming dissipating down the corridor, Mann sighed as he continued. "Commander."

"Yes Sire."

"I assume I don't have to remind you not to let him out of your sight? We cannot have him ruining our operation."

"No Sire."

"Maybe one day you can help me understand how he has so much favor with the people."

"He provides them much justification for their actions, my Lord. My apologies, I thought you knew?"

"Yes, Commander, thank you," Mann snipped back. "It was a rhetorical question. Now, anyway—all that aside, where were we? Yes—Ladies and Gentlemen of the War Council," he addressed the room. "Are you ready to do what needs to be done?"

"Yes Sire!" the chorused response filled the room.

"Well then, let us begin."

* * *

War was not new to Mann. In his time, much harm had been inflicted on him and his people. They had suffered, often to near ruin. But they had worked hard to repair. And with every hurt they had received, they had learned.

Each assault had been dreadfully horrid, yet, examining them in great depth, they had learned to make weapons of their own; smooth and pointy alike.

As agonizing for his beloved Citizens as it was, once studied and mused upon, a new hurt taught a great deal. Every cruel word and vicious lie hurled over the tops of his great City's walls, came with pain but was a curiosity to explore. Like the nasty jokes about his festive size spread by Friend City of Lorna in his second year at Newbury, or the clever way Tutor City of Carlyle in the Academy would belittle his every word to put him down. The tittering murmurs of the others' Interfacers when they thought he could not hear and every cruel sneer and taunt ever since. He remembered them all. The details each and every wound kept and cataloged in the grand galleries of the hall of records.

So when the Typist was called, he knew just what to do. Fabricated from the annals of the City's pain itself, his words were deadly. Clicking and clacking, the keys of his typewriter worked his craft. Truth, sawn in half, was ground till it was jagged. Dipped in vitriolic sulfur, gossip burned like fire. Slander was fused with malice, and honey flavored venom was labeled as humor and sweet gifts. Till, with a final 'ping', his deadly munitions were done.

Holding their anxious breath, the Politicians waited quietly until the couriers arrived. Where, each taking one of the crisp brown envelopes arranged in little piles on the desk, they left with their cargo that almost seemed harmless.

But it was not.

As they carried it through the empty streets to the City walls, the faint whispers of the grinning Feign who followed told them all they needed to know.

The Interfacers were waiting and they too, knew what to do. In pallid silence, the terrible sheets with the terrible words were handed out. One set for each of them laced with deadly intent. So reading the careful deceptions and committing them to heart, the dreadapults were loaded. And as the City reached its plotted destination, the order from high command was given.

I will spare you the horrors. Suffering and chaos are not things to be reveled in. But of the outcome you must know.

In careful shots, the first seeds of discontent were sown with his co-workers. Already their animosity towards authority was alive. Stoking the fire was easy.

City of Caspian did not really deserve his new role did he? Had he really worked for it like the rest of them? So young, so naive. He had not struggled like so many of them. He had been given the job, and rewarded the power. And for what? Experience? Hardly! He was born into affluence—this was not fair! This was not right!

For Caspian, there was something else. He listened well to the things that he liked. Thanks to his Idols of himself, he really believed that he was liked. He believed he was smart too. So liked and so smart that perhaps his lovely girlfriend City of Vera was not for him? Could he not do better? Especially now that he was Vice President—had she not been outgrown? Being so young and so handsome he had his whole life ahead, to be tied down seemed such a shame.

'But you know best Caspian, you're the boss!'

Sowing fear was just as easy.

'Did you hear the girls in accounting were laughing? You are quite young. But don't be so serious, it's just a joke.'

'But perhaps not? Maybe a little strong handedness will sort them out? A pay-cut or an exemplary firing? It is all part of the job, not a problem for you.'

Poor fool could be convinced of anything. But as the saying goes, an eye for an eye and a tooth for a tooth.

So unease spread and disquiet bloomed like a ravenous cancer. City of Caspian shed his lady love like a forgotten leaf. Mann had seen it since the start. She was good for him. She grounded him and kept him from his whims. Now she was gone.

His supporters turned on him. Friends became acquaintances and acquaintances became foes. His life became a war ground and his job became a toll. Until, one day he could take no more. And falling to his knees[31] in defeat, he resigned.

---

31. '. . . . . Oh my dear, sweet knees! How so very descriptive you are!! Without you I would be naught, wishing to divulge what I feel so deep yet cannot reveal with my face! Oh sweet gesture of my lower half—eyebrows of my legs! Knocking and falling, trembling and bending! Are there any limits to the many shades of your endless expression?!'

'L'art de la Reconnaissance' (The Art of Thankfulness) by Jean-Gaspard Pantameau. (ISBN 52-05-16/18)

Chapter 12

THE GREAT DEPRESSION OF MANN

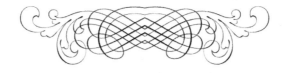

C omfort is a great and terrible thing.

In the near two hundred years that had passed since Caspian's defeat, City of Mann had flourished. Vice-President City of CitiCorp and then Division Director of all of Epicurea, his offices were some of the leading performers on the planet. Success brought with it much good, and in its bounty he had soaked up every warmth under the sun. Yet that is what was strange. Beyond the shroud of its contentment, all was not well.

Gazing out the window of the great hall as another dull explosion shook the Temple, Ruler Mann surveyed the smoldering expanse of his empire that lay before him.

'My beautiful City,' he sighed in dismay. 'What have we become?'

His empire lay in ruins. A great pyre of the lost.

'For how long have we waned?'

Distant sirens wailing, a helicopter flew close overhead and out into the fray, sending pillars of black smoke that rose from the streets curling beneath its shuddering rotors.

It had been months since the collapse began. Mann Financial was the first to go, followed by Spirit Bank and then City Capital. He should have seen it coming.

They told him it was alright, they told him it was nothing. The Temple was shining. Business was good. Crime was down and love for him, their glorious Ruler, was at an all time high. But deep down, he had known.

Burying his face in his hands he let out a silent scream.

He had known!

The Temple had shone. Of course it had—how could it not? Since the gold began to fade he had it entombed in mirrors and polished twice a day. But now it flickered like a dying ember, reflecting his City's pain as it burned.

Business was good because he had allowed it all.

'Eat and drink my beloved!' he had told them. 'For today you are alive!' But the gaunt stares of his citizens who looked back at him now were not those of the living, but rather of the starved—of those who tasted death.

Crime was down because he had judged and condemned, and cast all who fell short into prisons. And the ones he did not? Their love was not for him. Their love was for their Politicians and their comforts. He was but an afterthought, an abstract divinity. An apparitional embodiment of the improbable; luck and disaster, or the speculations of an unattainable paradigm. One who was—or was not. Who is—or is not.

Yet he had looked the other way. At first it stung. But it didn't matter to him! Of what significance were their whims or their thoughts, tossed like the waves of the sea? He was their Ruler. He was their king! It was he who was their champion, and he who had built this great City! The mighty Sentient City of Mann through which his great legacy would shine!

But in the many years that had passed, its wonders had grown strangely dim. He had searched for its fruit and yearned to lay hold of all it could give, yet nothing seemed to last. All seemed destined to be wasted away. The delights of his youth were now but empty laughter, and the fullness of his life as if filled with air.

Still, hungry for more, he had chased its every promise. Fine foods and friends were his joy. His strength was drawn from his companions and the wisest of Citykind. So for the many years of his devotion to knowledge, the name of his great City was spoken only with honor. With his grand assembly of towers and skyscrapers and his vast outer walls whitewashed like a brilliant pearl, his presence was a privilege. He had played at war and become the victor. He had played at peace and reaped its spoils—taking, as was his right, and giving, as was his righteous will. He had tried and he had won! Till all the comforts that the world could provide were his.

Yet, gazing out the window of the great hall, it was what it was. All for nothing—mere striving after wind. Slipping through his fingers like mist in the air. Doing nothing. Meaning nothing. Still a slave to the relentless march of decay. His City. His precious people. They had worked so hard—he had worked so hard! But when their purpose passed to memory, and their memory to myth—what then? Even if all that he had been was color and light—and it was not—it would soon pass. From the dust from which he came, he would return.

THE LORD OF
LORDS RESIDES

W hen your kind was first revealed to me it was a terror.

Humanity. Your shapes so odd and your functions so grotesque. Coughing, sneezing, oozing. So much biology crammed into such a tiny space. I winced at your supple forms, wondering how it was that you had survived. I laughed at the shortness of your lifespans and shuddered at how your people gave birth, revulsed by your leaky bodies and clammy skin.

'Oh odious, lodious[32] sight!' I lamented. 'For how long must I bear witness!'

I begged the one who showed me, to return me to my home. Yet he did not. And watching a thousand years of your spluttering horrors he showed me something else.

I watched as your kind grew to nations and as your nations were split by war. I watched as the dance of light and darkness played with the frailty of your fragile bones. And I watched, as time tumbled on—till I was led to know just one with whom whose life I was to become acquainted, and whom I would learn to love.

From birth I saw him grow. A seed of your kind. He drooled and dribbled, yet for his laughter I looked past my disgust.

"Oh huzzah, little human!" I praised, as he took his first steps and, "Bravo fine fellow!" as he graduated from school.

---

32. Lodious

(loʊdɪəs) ADJECTIVE

- A repulsive, repugnant or extremely unpleasant person or thing: ICKY

His underside was a lodious spectacle.

- (archaic) A specialized tool used to clean the internal cavity of a City's vacuum tube.

In the blink of an eye he had aged, becoming rich and raising children to reap the rewards of his life. Yet at night I heard his whispered tears. Tears that were familiar to me. For what does it profit a man, if he gains the world but loses his soul?

So, as his little graying head was laid to rest and his form returned to the dirt, I bade farewell. And I, the friend he had never known, was overcome with grief.

But you, watcher of mine, you know that this is not the end.[33] As you have learned.

You know of the rise and fall of the clouds, the ebb and flow of the tide. You know of roots and branch and structure. The true nature of the natural things. You know of them all.

Of seed and destruction, and where one must end for the other to begin.

---

33. As you have very cleverly noticed that there are still so many pages yet to turn.

Chapter 13

O' DARKEST NIGHT

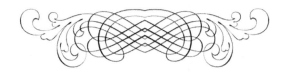

Beneath the window of the great hall, the thick red carpet where Ruler Mann stood was worn thin.

"My Lord?" Gibald asked softly as he approached. "Is there anything I can do for you before I turn in for the night?"

As Mann exhaled, the long velvet curtains rippled with his despondent breath.

"No," he sighed. "But thank you, Gibald. I don't know what I would do without you."

"Of course, Sire, it is my pleasure. If you need anything else, just ring the bell."

"Thank you, Gibald. Good night."

"Good night."

The sound of his gentle steps filled the quiet as he headed towards the door.

"Gibald?" Mann added, pausing in hesitation.

"Yes my Lord?"

"Can I ask you a question?"

"Yes my Lord. Anything."

"How is it that you stay so calm during all of. . . you know. . . " casting a forlorn glance out the window, Mann lowered his head, "this?"

With a furrowed brow, Gibald stopped for a moment, before responding with a gentle softness in his eyes.

"These worries, my Lord..." he replied. "The reason I do not carry them is because they are not mine to bear. They are for the one whom I serve. The one much greater than me."

"Oh, I. . ." Taken off guard by Gibald's answer Mann did not quite know what to say. "I see. Well, I— Thank you, Gibald. That is kind of you to say."

"You're welcome Sire. Will there be anything else?"

"No, thank you. That is all. Sleep well. Goodnight."

"You too, Sire. Good night."

The last glimmer of daylight fading to dusk, Mann watched on as the dark of night turned his City to black. Dots of gold and scarlet glowing from distant fires, the occasional sounds of chaos trembled through the silence.

"How did this happen?" he whispered his heartfelt dismay. "For what provision does this serve? What purpose? They trusted me, depended on me, needed me. . . And I have failed them. I have failed them all."

Startled by a flash of light, a luminous ball of flame rose on the horizon followed by a dull thud of an explosion. Falling to the ground, Mann began to sob.

"Oh God! What did I do wrong? I tried so hard. I have built for their good, yet all they have is ruin. I have worked for their life, yet all I have brought is death. Oh God! If all that I am was more than chance and chaos—what was your purpose? If I am truly your creation, what was your aim?! Can't you see my misery?! Can't you hear my pain?!! Why would you abandon me!!! WHY WOULD YOU LEAVE ME ALONE!!!!!!!

Screaming his anguish into the air with a mighty blast, the chambers of the great hall shook as Mann finally let it all go. Windows shattering into a million pieces, chairs and tables flew through the air, exploding in splinters against the walls. Chandeliers falling from the ceiling, the tapestries on the wall caught ablaze. As outside, cracks ran up the side of the Temple leading to a seismologist three miles away having the most exciting night of her career.[34] And as Mann crumpled into a ball of defeat, he buried his face in his hands.

"Please," he whimpered. "Help me, O God. I don't know where to turn. If you can hear me, show me what to do. . . I need your help."

34. From 'Unmasking Perception' Vol. 3: Great Inventions, Chapter 8 - The Seismograph: The Helena Seis Story
(ISBN 35-02-01)

'Twas a balmy Twaddlesday eve' when it happened. Again, the beastly sounds of my slumbering husband chastened me from sleep. So, when I could bear no more, I rose and padded across the creaky floor of the downstairs hall to my study.

Taking my seat before my seismograph, I watched as the delicate needle trailed its steady mark of peace on the papered cylinder. In my fifty two years of watching I had often wondered; Will it ever change from its silent state? Should maybe I have picked another career? Some said I was mad; the quakes had never happened, mere tales all based on myth. Some claimed they were rich imaginings of a simple mind. A delusional chimera, crafted to bridge the gaps in cognition of what one could not yet understand. Why some even said it was the tremors from the voice of an invisible ruler or angry spirit! But whatever it was, it was real. For I had felt one myself as a child while I played in the barn and had met others too, who had felt the same power as me. So as I sat in wait my awe was as new as the first. And when at last the earth moved again and my machine sprang to life, I was filled with glee.'

Chapter 14

THE LORD OF LORDS RESIDES

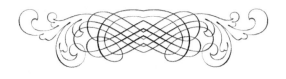

"Mann."

Like the rustle of autumn leaves, Mann jolted from his sorrow as the whisper of a still small voice breathed through the silence.

"Mann."

Sitting up straight and scanning around the destruction of the empty room, he brushed away his tears with his sleeve.

"Wake up, little one," it spoke again.

"Who said that?" he called out, as the tingle of panic rippled down his skin. "Who's there?"

Still quiet, but rising as if carried by a tempestuous wind, this time as it spoke, it rumbled like distant thunder. And though the room was indeed empty as its reply trembled through the air, they were so close that he felt their warmth on his skin.

"I am," it said.

Mann's breath stopped short as his heart thumped in his chest, "W—who are you?"

"I am the one who heard your cry."

"My cry?. . ." Staring out at the invisible presence, he stuttered as he choked back his fear. "Then you are him."

"I am."

Pausing in stifled silence, Mann was lost for words, "I. . . My Lord— I. . . I do not know what to say. I did not think you would come."

"But you hoped I would," the voice replied with a twinkling smile. "And that was enough."

Hesitating as his scrambled thoughts tried to order themselves in his head, Mann rubbed his eyes and looked around. "My Lord?"

"Yes Mann."

"May I ask a question."

"Anything."

"I do not mean to be rude but...where are you? How do I know that I have not just at last gone mad? You are but a voice in my ears. I cannot see you at all."

"I know, child. That is why I am here. I have come to show you everything. But do not worry. All will be revealed in time and I can see you well."

"Really?" Mann replied, slightly confused. "Why do you call me child then? Can't you see that I am aged in years? If you could see me, you would see that I am a wretch. I am near one thousand years old."

"Your age means nothing to me. It is but the blink of an eye. And besides—your form is the very least of what you are. I can see all of you; every hair on your head, and your every thought and desire to the very depths of your heart."

Pausing as his chest tightened, Mann lowered his head and glanced down at the floor. "My heart?. . . If you can see me that well, then you must see that your time is wasted. If you could see what I am, I. . . I am sorry. And I am sorry to waste your time. But please, leave me alone."

"Lift your head, little one. For I can also see that you do not yet know the fullness of who I am. For if you did, you would know I did not come to be your judge. I came to give you rest."

Rest. A word Mann had long since felt the meaning of. And as the loss of its distant memory stung his heart with sorrow, he hung his head in dismay.

"My Lord. . . If you have truly seen all I have done. You would not be able to look at me. . . I am so sorry. I have made such a mess."

As if in memory, the voice took a deep breath before exhaling with a sigh of sympathy, "Oh little one. But I have seen. And I do know. That is what I have come to show you. It is you who know nothing of me. Remember the hope in which you cried to for help. If I am even a shadow of who you hoped me to be, you would know that my love for you knows no bounds. For if I am God, then I am the God of Hope—nothing that I am has limits. And if I am God, I am all power, all knowledge, and all love; in whom all provision for all good has already been made. So if I am him, of course you have fallen short—all have fallen short. But you would also know that in the boundless depths of my love for you, I have given my life in your place so I can bring you home. It is done, little one. I did not come to condemn you. The price of your debt has already been paid.[35] I came to give you life and set you free."

"My Lord, I—" Struggling to contain the tears welling up in his tummy, Mann swallowed and gazed up toward the unseen presence. "I do not know if I. . . Your words are kind, but I do not understand."

"I know," the voice replied softly. "Come. Take my hand. Let me show you."

Feeling the gentle grasp of a hand on his, Mann rose to his feet. But before he had a chance to blink, he was pulled upward through the Temple roof. High into the sky above and across the City, they tore over the billowing stacks of the industrial district and past the regal grounds and spires of Academia that glinted in the first rays of the morning sun. He had never moved at such speed, and worried that he might let go he squeezed as tight as he could. But in an instant they were already slowing, and reaching the edge of Worthington's suburb they began to descend upon a little brick house, second to the last of a row of ten.

Topped with a red tile roof and painted a buttermilk yellow, it was small and worn. Yet for what it lacked in stature, it made up for in care. Led inside by the voice, Mann cautiously looked around at its neat and tidy interior. The tiny bathroom was clean and smelled of sweet soap. The dainty little kitchen was arranged with a neat bouquet of freshly cut flowers. Every room had a touch of kindness, and all were adorned with pretty pictures of happy times. But as the faint sound of a soulful lullaby drifted in from outside, he stopped and turned his head to listen.

"That is beautiful," he said, in awe of its soothing melody. "What is it?"

"It is the sound of love," the voice replied. "Do you want to see?"

Mann nodded.

"Come then."

---

35. For more information on this subject, please refer to your local planetary translation of the Intergalactic Sacred Book of Books, ref. Number: 43-03-16/18. (Book 43 of 66, Section 03, Line 16-18)

The scent of clean clothes clinging to the wind, Mann followed the voice into the garden. Strung on lines from one end to the other, white sheets and linens bobbed back and forth and as he looked amongst the fluttering fabrics towards the enchantment, he saw a Citizen, adorned in a flowing floral dress, singing in reverence as she filled a basket by her side.

"Who is she?" Mann whispered under his breath, being careful not to frighten her.

"It is alright. She does not know we are here. Come and see. I will show you."

Again, as before, the warmth of his guide's hand squeezed and he was ripped from his feet. But this time it was faster, with such a violence that for a moment he thought he might be torn apart. Then he was still. He could not bear to look, yet, as panic seemed ready to crush his chest, the voice continued in perfect calmness.

"Open your eyes."

Struggling to swallow through the lump in his throat, Mann cautiously peered out.

They were on the edge of a yawning chasm, and gazing out on the strange sight it was unlike anything he had ever seen. As if submerged in a great ocean of pure warmth, all glowed bright with soft and muted pinks. Dancing peach and apricot, the light shimmered soft with peaceful embrace, not a cavern of rock or earth, but alive. An organism. Breathing and pulsing. Swaying and flowing in placid harmony to the tranquil melody of the Citizen's lullaby that seemed to tremble from all directions, as it called its sweetness from beyond the ether.

"What is this place?" Mann started, but as faint movement caught his eye, he stopped short.

Massed in the chamber's center a mysterious object—a creature —turned and moved. Darker than its surroundings, it too was hued in delicate shades of pink, and as it rolled again it let out a rhythmic tremor from its center that thrummed in a fragile beat.

"What is that?!" he gasped.

"Listen," the voice replied. "He hears the call of his mother."

As if responding to the infants beating heart, the sweet song of the lullaby echoed in response.

"Mother?"

A sudden glimpse of the familiar caught his breath. A hand, complete with little fingers, and then a foot with some tiny toes. And as the creature turned towards his mother's voice, he gazed upon the tiny face of an unborn child.

Tension rising in his chest, transfixed by the fantastical vision, Mann was terrified.

"Do not be afraid," the voice spoke, giving his clammy hand a gentle squeeze. "I am with you."

"I. . . I have never seen such a thing," he whispered through shallow breaths. "How is this possible?"

"With me, all things are possible."

"Yes, but this. . . This is. . ." Tearing his gaze from the child, Mann turned to the voice, pausing as he struggled to find the words. "Why have you brought me here?"

"I wanted you to see a shadow of how I have made things to be. Tell me, when you look out there, what do you see?"

"What do I see? I— I don't know. A child, a. . . a Citizen— unborn in its mother's womb."

"And what is its purpose?"

"Its purpose? To grow, I suppose. In this. . . place. It is his home."

"And how does he grow? Does he work hard, or make plans or worry?"

"What?" Mann chuckled. What a funny thought. "No. How could he? Look at him, he's— All he has to do is rest and feed until it is time to go."

"Go? Time to go where?"

"You know, go out there." Squinting upward he pointed to the luminous glimmer of the world beyond. "He cannot stay here forever, right?"

"But why would he want that? All that he needs is right here."

"For now, yes. But this place is only temporary. It won't last forever. Out there is where he belongs. His real purpose is to be with his family and to be a Citizen of my City."

"Maybe so. But he does not know that. Look at him. He is an infant in existence. What does he know of out there in the world beyond this place? He has never seen more, or been told more. To him, this place is everything—his universe. All that there was, all that there is, and all that there ever will be. In his mind, there is nothing else. How could there be? Where is the proof that he can see with his half open eyes, or the evidence he can touch with his tiny hands? Here, he has it all and knows it all. There is no more. And here, in this place, in his palace—he is king. Why would he want to leave?"

"But he can't stay here? Is the end of his time here not inevitable?"

"It is. But he does not know what is next. Tomorrow is but a concept. Here and now is all that he knows and all that he can comprehend. Should he not just eat and drink and enjoy all that he has now? And what of more? If this is all there is and more is what he wants, should he not have it? Is it not his right? Surely all that is stopping him from becoming lord of this universe is his own lack of control? Is his body not his own? Does it not wiggle and flex to his command? So why not this world? Should he not be lord of this place too and master of how it forms and grows? Surely this world should be his to sculpt in any way that he pleases. He should be king of all it will allow. But how? Should he cut that chain that shackles him by his little belly? It holds him against his will! And then he would be free to roam this place as its god!"

"What?" Mann laughed, bemused by the images of the little king playing out in his head. "But that would kill him! For as amusing as it is, I do not think he would survive."

"But why then, does he not do these things? Why does he not even try?"

"I don't know?! He just. . . he just doesn't. I do not know if he even thinks of such things. All his cares are with his mother. I think he is quite happy to keep his fate in her hands."

As if in agreement, the baby outstretched its tiny arms into a wide yawn before curling back into a ball.

"He is, isn't he," the voice smiled. "And yet he barely even knows her. He has never seen her face or known the warmth of her gentle touch. And yet, resting solely in the hope of her perfect provision and perfect love, his desire is to be with her, an existence he cannot fathom, in a place he cannot comprehend. So, as he hears her call that she sings to him now, when the end comes for this place and the waters break, he will not fight or cling to the walls. For he clings to his hope in his provider."

For a moment, they stood quiet and admired the serenity of the creature's peaceful existence. It was all so strange. Yet it was real. Feeling the strength of the hand that held his, Mann felt calm and looking up at the face of the voice that guided him, he was at peace.

"My Lord," Mann asked. "Can I ask you a question?"

"Anything."

"You say you are all this for me?"

"Yes. I am."

"Well what must I do for it to be done?"

"No more than him, little one," the voice continued. "As he believes in the one who provides for him, all you must do is believe in me who has provided everything for you."

"And that is it?"

"Yes. That is it. Everything else will be added, and I will guide you every step of the way."

Glancing down at his feet Mann paused as he thought. "My Lord?"

"Yes Mann?"

"I do."

So it was done. And clinging to the hope[36] in which he believed, Mann was taken upward with a tug on his hand.

Ascending skyward through the womb, the woman in the garden of the little yellow house vanished to a speck below. And drifting far above the burning sprawl of his empire across the City, he returned to the Temple, floating through the ceiling of his chambers to where he was tucked beneath the soft down quilts of his bed.

"My Lord?" he asked sleepily, as the candle blew out and the door began to close.

"Yes, Mann," God replied.

"Will I see you tomorrow?"

"You will. From this day on, we will never be apart."

"Oh, I see. . . But will you be, like—you know—here?"

"Yes, My Child. For as you have made your home with me, I have made my home with you."

"Oh. And my Lord?"

"Yes Mann?"

"One more thing. Can you leave the door open a bit? I like to see the light from the hallway."

"Of course, little one."

"Thank you."

"You are most welcome. Now get some rest, tomorrow is the first day of the start of your life. Goodnight Mann. And sweet dreams."

---

36. I don't know Billy. Sometimes I feel as though I am losing hope. Seeing Mummy so deathly ill like this makes me terribly sad."

"I know," he replied, resting his little hand on hers. "Me too. But it will get better. I just know it will. Besides, Grandma Eleanor says we can't lose hope. She said we can only hide from it. She says it's all around us, and even inside us."

"Inside us!," Susie giggled. "Like even in our tummies?! Well that *is* funny. What in heaven's name did she mean by that?"

"Well, she said that we were never meant to put limits on hope as we often do, but we are instead supposed to hope for the highest in all things as it was intended."

"Like for two birthday presents instead of one?"

"Well yes—but I think much, much, more than that. She called it hope eternal. She said to keep adding hope onto hope, until hope itself becomes the one doing the adding! Then it will be hope itself who shows you where it leads."

"I'm not quite sure I understand."

————-continues on the next page————-

"Well, like when you said two birthday presents; why not hope for more? Whatever you want and as many as you want. More and more, over and over until you have all the things you could possibly think of; all the things that exist and all the things that ever will exist. But just because you have it all, you don't stop there. You keep going. Hope for more. Past material things and money, you hope for health and happiness and cleverness, and the ability to only make good decisions. And then you keep hoping. Now not for yourself, but for others. You hope the same for family and friends, for their perfect future. Yours and theirs and all those after you, your children and your children's children. On and on, until your name and your kin and your kind have filled the universe. But again, you don't stop there. Surely legacy and memory is not your final hope? When time and existence itself comes to an end, who will there be left to remember?!—So what do you do?"

"I don't know. Hope?"

"Now you're getting it! Yes, you hope—you hope some more! You hope for a life after death. A place beyond this place that transcends the fetters of this realm. But then more. For your hope is not for tears or sadness, but joy and peace! Love that never ends. So hoping past the limits of our goodness and wisdom, you hope for something else. Someone else. One that will never let you down, one who will never fail. Who is all knowing. All powerful. Pure in power and pure in love; a goodness ruling above all things. Watching, waiting, wanting for you—his creation, his little one—to return to his eternal embrace. And in that moment as your hope rests in your Creator, the creator of your hope, the embodiment of your hope—you see that the very hope in which you were calling for him, was in fact him calling for you."

For a moment the pair sat in silence, contemplating the thoughtful words.

"Do you think she'll live for much longer?" Susie asked.

"Who? Mummy?"

"No, Grandma Eleanor."

"Oh. No. I wouldn't think so. She is rather old. Father said he would be surprised if she survives the winter."

– From 'The Children of Rigsby Manor' by Susan B. Ertworth
(ISBN 54-01-01)

Chapter 15

THE FIRST DAY

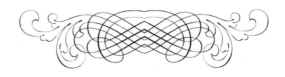

<u>Morning</u>

Mann's eyes opened.

What was that?

A tremble ever so slight reverberated through the floor. Cuddled beneath the sheets, he stared blankly at the ceiling.

There it was again.

A rumble shook the bed and a picture fell off the wall.

What was that?!

Alarmed, he sat up and looked around. But before he had a chance to shout for help, the hand of an earthquake deep beneath the City rocked the ground.

With a mighty roar the whole room shook. Cracks ripped the ceiling sending chunks of plaster tumbling to the floor. Furniture screeched as it moved and the terrified screams of all the City's Citizens echoed through the Temple's halls.

And then it stopped.

The early morning sun streaking through a gap in the curtains, Mann sat still with his blanket pulled tightly around him. What was that? His heart pounding in his chest, he did not move. Yet as the dust began to settle his shock soon turned to memories of the night before. What in tarnation was going on?!

Suddenly, the door flew open. "Code red, my lord!!!!" Gibald yelled as he burst into the room, "Code redddd!!!!"

"Gibald!" Mann replied, "what has happened?! Are you alright?!"

"Lord Mann, wake up!! It's a code red! There was an earthquake and it has split the City and opened up the ground!!"

"An earthquake?!!" Mann exclaimed, throwing off sheets aside as he leapt out of bed. "This cannot be!! What about the Citizens?! Is anyone hurt?!"

"I do not know my lord! The City is in chaos! The earth has cracked and there is water and rivers, and trees! All has gone mad! The people have gone into code red!! And the Constitution, my lord!! It has been written with a new law!! What do we do!!!!"

"Rivers and trees?! Calm yourself Gibald! You are making no sense!!**37**

"I know my lord! I'm sorry! But you do not understand— Look!"

Shaking as he pointed at the bedside table, Gibald fell silent as Mann followed his outstretched finger and looked. Then he furrowed his brow and looked closer.

How peculiar?

Etched on the top, as it too was etched on the drawers and handles and everywhere else for that matter—the familiar words of the Constitution were clear. But they were not quite familiar, as indeed, something had changed. In neat gold letters written over all the others, there was a new command that simply said:

LOVE ONE ANOTHER AS I HAVE LOVED YOU

Catching his breath, Mann recoiled in surprise.

"How is this possible?" he whispered to himself.

---

37. Taken from, 'Herman Gets a Haircut.' - Puzzled Kids Publications (ISBN 46-02-09)

Herman could hardly contain himself.

'What a peculiar thing to believe!' he sniggered to himself, squashing a smile breaking the corner of his mouth. 'How hilarious! A God who created the whole world and watches over us? Why, that is the silliest thing I have ever heard!'

He did not mean to be rude, but the rising strain of mirth tickling his belly was almost unbearable. It was all too funny. So fighting to keep a straight face, he stood up from the pew and spluttering with amusement excused himself from the church.

Down the aisle as quick as he could and bursting out the doors into the warm desert air, the great pangs of merriment trapped in his chest almost hurt. Hopefully no one inside could hear, but it didn't matter. It was too late. Exploding in an uncontrollable spasm of laughter, tears streamed down his face as his whole body shook with glee, *Do the limits of people's imagination have no bounds!!! How utterly absurd!!'*

Choking on great guffaws of chuckles he crossed the dusty road and reaching the four legged aggregation of organic tissue and pumping biological mass he called 'horse', he threw his leg over the saddle. Then, passing the mixture of gasses he had captured in his chest cavity over the tissues in his throat he had expertly shaped, he guided the sound-waves that were created into very specific noises with his tongue. "Come on, girl!" they reverberated. "Let us leave this ridiculous place behind and go home."

The horse understood. Capturing the sound in the side of her head and converting it into electricity (she had received these electrical signals before and had come to learn what it was that the creature on her back meant) and producing new electrical signals of its own, she began to contract and relax various bits of her body, propelling them forward through the billions of invisible particles and waveforms that bombarded their bodies. And as they hurtled through the cosmos at thousands of miles per hour by the enormous mass of solid and liquids that spun beneath their feet, they were warmed by the flaming ball of plasma that hovered in the sky.

"That is what I was trying to say, my lord," Gibald continued shakily. "And it's not just this one, it is all of them. Every constitution from here to the outer walls!"

"All of them?! But how? Wait. . ." Pausing in thought, flashes of the night before came rushing back. "Of course! Gibald— I think I might know why all this has happened. Tell me again about these rivers and trees. What do they look like?"

"Tell you? I would Sire. But I am afraid my words will only fail. This is something you need to see."

<u>Afternoon</u>

Gibald was not wrong. The change etchings on the constitution had affected every one. Each and every one now glowing bright with the same seven words.

He was not wrong about the code red either. It was a code red. And as Mann tore through the Temple at breakneck speed, he could hear the frozen terror of his Citizen's panic shriek through the eerie silence.

"Help us lord Mann!" they cried with their minds from every corner of the City. "Save us!!"

Outside in the courtyard, the deathly quiet screamed with their discomfort too, "Please, good king! Save us all!!"

Over the pool of cleansing towards the golden gates, he hurtled past the altar which had split and cracked. Yet perched above his empire at the top of the white marble steps, he was not prepared for what he saw next.

Stopping in his tracks he stared in amazement at his City. Gibald was not wrong about it either. For in all the change he had seen in his City, this was a new kind.

From beneath the Temple steps, a surge of crystal water had erupted in an ethereal cloud, where, roaring as it cascaded down the hill, it frothed and foamed as it rushed towards the waiting streets. Yet just as it reached the first houses, it slowed and split, with each branch calming to a steady flow.

Four in all, they were rivers indeed, but like none he had ever seen. Majestic as they were gentle, they were pure as the sapphire blues of heaven, and as they purposefully meandered their way through the City, their blissful surface twinkled like scattered diamonds in the sun.

The urgency of his people's cries growing louder, Mann leapt into the sky and sped towards the closest one. And as the streets and houses flickered past below he approached the river's edge. Yet slowing, puzzled he drew a breath.

'How could it be?'

It had not even been an hour since the earth had moved yet the riverbanks were already fully formed. Rich with lush green pastures and tall with strong swaying trees, flowers of every color bloomed and creatures of every kind had flourished. Birds sang, butterflies fluttered, and livestock was grazing to their heart's content—all in living praise to the water that brought them to life.

Mann did not know what to think. It was magnificent. It was marvelous—yet it was all too much. The anguished dread of his Citizens still screaming in his mind, his head was beginning to hurt and the bleat of their need had given him a terrible thirst.

Drifting to a patch of soft grass by the river's edge, he dropped to his knees and closed his eyes. The sweet sounds of the water babbled and swirled as a cool breeze drifted over him as if whispering its peaceful calling. He was so tired. So filled by the sound of its stillness, he dipped his cupped hands beneath the icy water, and drank.

And it was nice.

Better than nice—it was good. It was very good. All still, all clear, all calm. And in sudden crystal clarity, he understood what he was to do.

Like a clap of thunder he leapt from the ground, and speaking with the voice of a storm, every Citizen in the City looked as he soared into the air.

"Citizens of Mann!" he bellowed. "Come and drink! This water is for you!"

In an instant, the sea of pleading voices in his head vanished and the City descended into silence. But only for a moment, as with the simple twinkle of a single nod, the collective voice had been sparked. Quickening in fervor and rising in energetic tone, soon it was blazing as it spread like wildfire in every direction— with nervous excitement to start, but then with happiness and joy!

The elated cheers of his beloved people erupting across his City, Mann watched in delight as they poured out of their homes. Filling the streets, there were thousands of them, tens of thousands, hundreds of thousands—marching and dancing in unison across the riverbank's verdant plains. And with a splash in the river's clean waters, it was the children who ran in first. Then their mothers and fathers and uncles, sisters and friends! All sorts of every kind! Laughing as they played and singing as they swam!

"My beloved children!" Mann declared, the tempestuous force of his words washing over every surface and shaking the ground. "Sweet Citizens of the City of Mann! Hear my words!"

"Yes lord!" the collective shout of his people replied as they heard. "We are listening!"**38**

---

38. They weren't.

"This water is not from me—It is from someone else. One of whom I am not even worthy to untie his shoe!"**39**

The mutters of their million awestruck noddings rustled like trees in the wind.

"No longer are you to call me lord, no longer are you to call me god and no longer are you to call me king! I am not!! We are not!!! For I have seen the one who is greater; the one who is above us all. The true Lord! The God of gods! The King of kings! And to him I have given my rule! He is the Lamb and the Lion! The Creator of it all!! And today, I bring you good news! He has come to live with us all!!"

39.
'Allison' - A Biography of the Queen of Mercia by Reginald B. Tardale

Indeed the highest form of flattery, stating one's 'unworthiness to even untie another's shoe' had always been second to none in terms of compliments. Queen Mercia thought she would never tire of hearing it. Yet it was not until her seventh month of pregnancy that she realized its limitations.

Struggling even to see her feet over her protruding belly she would protest. "Please!" she exclaimed, "I cannot reach!"

But her servants and maidens would just blush at her request. And the more she begged the more they loved her for being a truly humble Queen.

"Never, my Queen!" they would reply, "We are far from worthy of such a noble task!"

So whether in bed, or in the bath; for six long weeks she was a prisoner in her own shoes.

Evening

After the excitement of the day's festivities the Great Hall seemed quieter than usual, and standing cautiously in the open doorway, Mann was a little nervous.

"My Lord?" he called out. "Are you here?"

"I am, my child," the voice of God replied. "Come in. I was just cleaning up."

He had been cleaning up. Paintings and tapestries restored, everything was back in its proper place, all fixed and cleaned and polished. The chandeliers were mended and the broken windows were repaired as good as new. With marble floors gleaming, the air smelled like flowers with a hint of fresh paint, and as Mann drifted up the red carpet towards the throne, he looked around in awe.

"Over here," God's voice rang out from behind him.

"Eeeek!" Mann squealed as he spun around with fright.

"Here, little one. By the window."

"I am sorry, I thought you were on the…"

"It is quite alright. You will get used to it. You can see me by the light that shines from me—See?"

Mann could see. Floating towards the tall window that overlooked the City, the walls, floor and ceiling glowed as if lit from every direction at once.

"How did you sleep?" God continued. "Do you feel a little better?"

"Me? My Lord, I slept like I died and was born anew! But it does not matter—I have seen the waters of your river! I saw the life it brings; the pastures and the trees and—my Lord. Thank you, I. . . I do not know what to say."

"You are welcome, my child," the words shimmered with a smile. "I am glad you like it."

"Oh, I do, my Lord! Please, there must be something I can do to repay you?"

"I would only ask that you share what I have given you with the world. Did you see the new law that I have written in gold?"

"Of course!" Mann chuckled. "It would be hard to miss that!"

"Good. Well if you wish to give thanks, that is how. Simply obey."

"That is it? But. . . surely there must be something else I can do?"

"There is not, little one. That is it."

A silence lingering between them, Mann pondered the words of the new law. That shouldn't be so hard. Love others just as much as. . . how does that work? All others? Is there room for mistakes? Opening his mouth to ask a question, he stopped short, as the rumble of a distant explosion shook the floor. Turning in shock his heart sank, and as he stared out the window he watched in dismay, as a fireball rose over the City.

"No!" he cried out. "This can't be!! What are they doing?! My Lord! I was just with them! Please! Do something! I told them everything! They were playing in the water and eating of the fruit!! Stop you fools!" he yelled, hammering on the glass with his fist. "STOP!!"

As the echo of another shuddering blast rumbled through the room, Mann stepped back in disbelief as a second bloom of violence mushroomed on the horizon.

"Oh Lord! What have I done wrong? I showed them everything and told them everything they had to do! Why are they doing this?"

The crackle of BIA fighter jets thundering overhead, he choked on his words in stifled shock. But just as he thought he might be sick, God took a gentle hold of his trembling hand.

"Be still, little one. There is purpose and provision for them too."

"But where is the purpose in this?!" Mann pleaded, "Please, they are hurting! Just tell me what to do to make them change!"

"Do not be worried for them, I know each one of them by name. They are not forgotten. Do you believe that it is my will to heal them all?"

Mann paused. God did speak in the most peculiar way sometimes.**40**

"Yes," he said with a deep breath, "I do, but, I— I don't understand."

"Nor do they, child. Not yet. But if you stay close, in time you will. Come. Follow me—I will show you the way."

40. . . . . "But my dearest Tongue," scoffed Hands, throwing back his appendages in a mocking gesture. "Why the puzzlement and why the mysterious words? Why is it that this God you speak of, speaks in such a peculiar manner? Why does he seem to dabble in metaphor and dip into the abstract with his toes?"

"Because, how else?" Tongue replied. "Remember how difficult it was when you and I met? You telling of roughness and smoothness, and I, of tart and sweet."

"Ha, yes," he chortled. "It was an amusing courtship. But we were just six months old. I did not understand a word of what you were saying. Remember when we traveled to the Vale of Lilies and you ate a thorn?"

She giggled, "How could I forget! What a calamity! But do you see what I mean? I, being naive to how you worked in form and function did not know what it was you were trying to say. To me, 'Sharp' meant lemons or pickles, so I thought you were telling of how good it would be to eat! I may know better now, but back then the language of your existence was unknown to me."

"But I tried to warn you too!" Eyes chimed in. "Did I not say it looked rather pointy!"

"You did, dear Eyes, you did. But you too must see what I mean? For I, unknowing of your angles and shapes thought *you* meant 'pointy'—like hot pepper or horseradish! How was I to know? Only through much analogy and metaphor have I come to have a better understanding of what and how and who you are!"

'The Senses of Youth' by G.B. Harding
(Chapter 11: Ear Gets Cake in Him)

THE NEW CITY OF MANN

Now delightful!" you exclaim, leaping from the comfort of your seat and throwing your arms in the air. "How perfectly splendid! Everything is going to be alright! The City of Mann of whom I have become quite fond is going to make it!"

Sitting back down with a satisfied sigh, you turn to the final section of this book, curious as to how it will all end. It got heavy there for a while. So dark and morose and specific…And strange. So very strange. Perhaps Mann has gone mad?

But then, as the subdued curl of a smile breaks the corner of your mouth, you realize that it has to be specific! It has to be strange!

Are these not the ways of God, who transcends all, and provides all, in perfect provision? Specificity is a certainty in the ways of the all knowing. Vague or changeable cannot be a product of his plans. And as for strange? Of course they are strange. Are the ways of a mountain not strange to a mouse? Do we expect God to fit neatly within the confines of our intellect or to be bound by the limitations of our strength? Do we expect he can always be anticipated and always understood? By no means! In the humble, narrow eyes of the created, strange is a precept. For if we, mere infants in existence, can fully understand the ways of God, surely it is not God whom we claim to know? In the hands of the everlasting, we must expect the unexpected and revel in surprise.

Straightening up in surprise as you finish reading what you just thought, and then in further surprise, as you read this bit explaining your surprise at reading your thought, you turn your ruminant musings back to the world of the Great Sentient Cities, and the one known as Mann.

Chapter 16

THE WAR IS WON

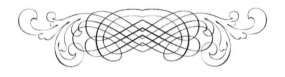

And so it was, with evening and morning, and the afternoon sandwiched in-between, that the first day of all the rest to come came to an end.

In the days that followed, the Lord of lords began his work in the City of Mann. He started in the Temple. And with Mann by his side and his light illuminating the way, they wandered through the many halls and corridors.

He spoke of many things. Wondrous things, marvelous things; of the limitless depths of his purpose and provision. Of his endless love and his perfect truth and the mysteries of reality itself. Of space and time, the end and the beginning, of realms and creatures unknown. Of how all had already been given. Of Earth, of mankind. Of the words they had received—and of his greatest gift to all creation; the Seed of his Favor. And as Mann nodded profusely, and heard how it was impossible for him to do anything by himself, he saw the Temple like he had never seen it before.

Frankly, it was a mess. Messier than even he believed. Where once he had seen only polished marble, scattered paper wrappers and empty containers littered the floor. Rooms were piled with bags of waste and walls were black with grease and slime.

He made excuses at first, yet eventually he had seen enough. Embarrassed and ashamed, he asked for it to be cleaned. And with a nod from the Lord of lords, it was done.[41]

It was the same for the Politicians and the Traders. They were his people—some were even friends—yet beneath the warmth of God's glow they were something else. Hissing through jagged teeth, they looked so different, growling with scarred and twisted scowls. Way deep down he wondered if he had known who they were before, yet just did not want to know. But seeing them as they were in the light, he could hardly bear to look. So hanging his head he said farewell, and asked for them to be driven out.

---

41. **Excerpt from, 'the Life and Times of the McCleary Temple Cleaning Service', by J.D. McCleary**

The business had been in my family for decades. Nine generations of McClearys in all. Cleaning was in my blood. But seeing how the Creator of the universe went about cleanin', I knew it was only a matter of time before I was out of business. Truth be told, as God illuminated the great heaps of rubbish that seemed to fill every corner, I remembered how it got there. Either by a Citizen or a Politician, and even the Spirit Ruler himself, they were all at it—just making a mess. No-one seemed to care. But until God shone his light, no-one could really see how bad it was neither.

My livelihood aside though—it did explain a lot. The rats. The smell. The poisonous drinkin' water and all them Citizens who were randomly getting sick. Maybe grandma McCleary was right? Maybe I should have gone to college like my cousin Alfie. But who could have guessed that the company would one day be competing against God himself?! Oh well. Too late now I suppose.

Together, hand in hand, they walked for days. Until all that was unclean in his sight was cleaned, and all who he saw to be unfit to stay were driven out. Yet there was much to learn.

The Temple was one thing, but flying over the ruins of the streets he knew so well was hard. Vivid reminders of his efforts and failures striped the ground. The smoldering husks of bombed out homes and the blackened scars of violence speaking loudly to what, by himself, he could never be. So turning to the Lord of lords who flew closely by his side, he again asked for help. But as God gave, it was not as he had expected.

Leading Mann to the banks of the River, he asked him to call a Citizen down to the water to drink. So he did. And with a gentle call into the wind, it was not long before one came.

A small little fellow with big ears—certainly not the handsomest or friendliest of his Citizens—as he kneeled by the waters edge, he grumbled to himself, something about how rude it was that his schedule was being interrupted.

Sniffing it first, he was quite suspicious, but then, dipping a finger into the water he examined it, before dabbing a drop on his tongue and raising his eyebrow to think. It did not take long for him to decide. Smacking his lips together and going back for more, it was clear that it was good. And in a moment more he was slurping with such vigor that it splashed all over his smiling face.

Mann was happy to see him drink, and watched him for a while. Yet it was only when he got up to leave, that Mann noticed that he glowed. From his hair and his eyes and his skin, the funny little fellow shone bright with a sparkling light. And as he strolled across the lush pastures of the riverbank, the radiance of his little body lit the path ahead.

'This is most unexpected', Mann thought to himself. So staying close behind, he followed him as he made his way home.

It did not take long. Ten minutes to the bus stop and then fifteen minutes more, the 701 Bodington glimmered with his new light as it rumbled along with him inside. And soon, as he waved to his perplexed neighbors who squinted at him marching up the driveway to his front door, he was there. Kicking off his shoes, he walked into the kitchen and then, taking a puzzled look around at the illuminated space, he wrinkled his nose and began to clean.

"By the girdled loins of Columbus!!"[42] Mann gasped. For by the River's light that the little fellow shone, he too could see the mess. The table was smeared with food, as were the counters and the chairs. The ceiling was dotted with thick black mold and the sticky floors piled high with trash. And that was just the kitchen.

---

42.   **Did you know?**

Although a common expression of the day, the phrase, 'by the girdled loins of Columbus', is nearly 12,000 years old!

In the height of the Talmerdian Empire, the ruler at the time, King City of Columbus IIX, became ill. An unfortunate malady that caused uncomfortable irritation on the undercarriage of his structure, he had a special girdle constructed for his parts that was coated in a medicinal salve.

Not wanting to appear weak before his vassal kingdoms however, he chose only to wear it at night, vowing all who knew of its existence to secrecy. Yet the secret did not remain secret for long.

Perhaps too amusing to keep quiet forever, soon the tales of its soothing comforts were spreading across the land, and before long the good King's loins were the talk of the kingdom. But then the unthinkable.

No one knows exactly how it began, but with a simple mixup of the letter 'L', the rumor changed. 'Girdled' became 'Girded', and hearing whispers that the King was girding his loins under cover of night, laughter turned to war.

Within six months from the start of his famous itchy underparts, the surrounding kingdoms had broken the treaty in a preemptive attack, and King City of Columbus and his girdled loins, was dead.

Trinkets and pictures lined the shelves and walls of every room, with idols of the things he worshiped and the writings of the things he yearned. Yet hour after hour, the Citizen cleaned, and losing strength as his light grew dim, he gave thanks to the Lord of lords and tucked himself into bed.

So as Mann followed, God showed him the way. And as God's perfect provision provided, he was provided with all of his every need. Leading his people to the water to drink, one by one his Citizens returned to peace. Till, in time, it brought an end to war. Factions crumbled, idols fell and were burned, and the banner of the Lord of lords was raised high above them all.

Chapter 17

THE BATTLE BEGINS

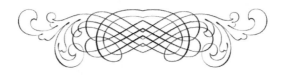

It was in this way that the war to end all wars came to an end. Marked with the new law and sealed by the one who set it in place, the Lord of lords was sovereign over City of Mann. Victory had been secured and the war was won. And in that simple conclusion all assurance was given.

Yet the battle for the City of Mann and his people had just begun. For just as when a seed sprouts a small green plant, new life has been received. But how it grows or the fruit it bears, depends on how it feeds.

The Will of the People

It was once said that, 'the Citizen is no help at all.'

Seeing how much his people could accomplish as a collective, Mann had always resented this idea. But with each day that passed since the Lord of lords had come to stay, he couldn't help but wonder if maybe the sayer of that saying was right.

His Citizens had never been particularly good at following the law, and even with the Creator of the universe in charge, they still did not really listen or obey. In fact, far from perfect and as peculiar, willful and silly as anyone can be, the extent to which his beloved little Citizens embodied these attributes seemed to have no limit.

Strangely quick to fall back into their old ways, it would seem that unless the words of the new law were clearly visible in their lives, they simply forgot. So much as they overlooked the old laws —for all their good intentions—it was not long before they overlooked the new.

But what of the cleaning, you say? Is this not why they walked down to the water to drink?

Well yes, it was. But of how they got there and of what good it did for them, they were quick to forget. When Mann came looking for them and told them of the River, they believed him. They rejoiced when they heard the news that he spoke. Yet within a day or so of quenching their thirst, they would wake one morning with no recollection of what happened at all. Finding the sparkling surfaces and organized shelves of the homes that they themselves had cleaned just days before, they would hypothesize in awe of how it happened. Mann of course, telling of the water and its light would take them back again to drink. But with another clean and a sleep, they would soon forget and go back to how they were before.

Then it would all begin again.

A dustball in the hallway and some crumbs on the carpet. Then a spilled chocolate milk or dropped tv dinner. One thing added to another, until it was very messy indeed. And once more, as the words of the Constitution were covered, they lost sight of what it said. And you know what happens next. A knock on the door, as fixation, obsession, fancy and craze came calling; and invited in, in they came.

Though it was not just the Citizens who were forgetful who caused an issue. Some of them were stubborn too. Peculiar and silly also, the stubborn were as forgetful as the rest, and sitting down for breakfast a day or so after a good clean, they too would gaze puzzled at the pristine twinkle of their kitchens. But coupled with a bullish hate of change, of returning to the idols of their old ways they were much more prone.

Before their trip to the River you see, they had been quite happy with their lives—happier still with their infatuations—and the idea of change to these rascally fellows was not appealing in the least. Like the forgetful, breaking a habit to try something completely new was exceedingly hard. But in their little minds, quite content with all their comforts, to make any change at all was a terrible idea. So as Mann came calling the good news, they would go to great lengths to avoid what he had to say.

Some would pretend he wasn't there, whistling and inattentively looking around while he spoke, while others would run away as quickly as they could. Doing everything in their power to avoid him, often in the most masterful way. Utilizing every brazen plan and sneaky ploy in the book,[43] they would abandon bicycles, hide in sewers and leap off moving trains, risking life and limb in their quest to get away. So whether he was pleading to them just to listen, or tickling one who was playing dead, it was never easy. But for all the resistance they put up they were not the hardest of his people to deal with. Because for all their faults—at least they didn't bite.

Biters were the third kind of Citizen that Mann had to contend with. Called biters for a reason, biters were void of any will to change at all. And as well as being stubborn and forgetful, they were mean.

Mann had never noticed them in his City before, but then again, that was before the Creator of the Universe had come to stay. (Things had gotten weird since then.) In appearance, for all anyone could tell they were normal, upright Citizens. Yet on hearing him call them to the River their whole demeanor would change. Not running or hiding or any of those things that the stubborn would do, they would just look to the sound of his voice

---

43.

Dating back tens of thousands of years to the dawn of Sentient Citykind, 'The Sneaky Brazen Ploy Plan Book' is one of the oldest texts in Citykind's existence.

Still as relevant today as it was when it was written, it is a fascinating and comprehensive collection of reasons, excuses and practical methods that enables Citizens to do and think nothing outside of their close surroundings and immediate future.

Acclaimed by many Citizens across the planet for helping them through their short little lives, it has been hailed as the gold standard of existential comfort.

Published by Ranthom Bodgins, The Sneaky Brazen Ploy Plan Book Volume 12 is now available in 73 different languages in most major retailers planet-wide.

and glare. And if he approached them!!! Have you ever said something to someone that you thought was kind, interesting or even helpful, only to have them erupt in a verbal tirade? It was like this with the biters. But at the mention of the River, their response was a teeth-filled rage!

How they reacted was confusing and painful. Mann did not understand. They were his Citizens and he just wanted to do them good. But they would not do what they were told. He asked the BIA to help as well, but to no avail. Other than adding bitemarks to their uniforms they achieved no more than him. So, after braving the wrath of their displeasure many times, he gave up on them and left them alone.

The Will of the Politicians

The Politicians were different. From the day they were removed from the Temple, they embraced the change and vowed to never forget. Preaching what they knew to be true, they quickly found new homes amongst their voters and continued to do what they did best.

"Change has come!" they said. "Change for the good of all!"

Telling of the Lord of lords and his power, they spoke with such eloquence and confidence. Of how the City would be transformed and how the Citizens would be saved. And although they had lost the prestige of the Hall of Sanctum, for them, a soap box on a corner or a park bench was more than enough. In some areas it even seemed to be better. Drawn by impassioned speeches and colored words, crowds grew throughout the districts to listen to what they had to say.

Mann was delighted. Biters aside, the Citizens numbered in the tens of millions, most of which were forgetful or stubborn. So even with his incredible speed and the tremendous sound of his voice, the task of telling his people the good news was daunting. But with his Politicians by his side they would never forget! To the River they would take them, drawing the crowds to the long grass and flowers of its banks to tell them its wonders as they cooled by the fruit trees in the shade. Yet this was only at first. Watching them closely, something was amiss.

For of all the many things that the Politicians spoke, they would never mention that the waters of the River were for the Citizens to drink. Not once. Listening closely you would hear 'splash' and 'swim' and 'play' and 'dance', but never 'drink'. And listening closer still, you would find they only praised who they praised before.

King Quantis preached of the glorious numbers,[44] and the marvelous projections of the City's better future were proclaimed by Lady Wanting of the Wandering Eye.

---

44. Precisely one decimal second (1 / 174900 of a Sentient City day) after the Lord of lords came to stay, King Quantis of Currencia identified a new metric and quickly set to work in understanding how the City may benefit from its use. A means of measuring how godly the City was, expressed as units of Piet (pU), it was without a doubt a revolutionary discovery with applications ranging an improved sense of superiority, an improved sense of wisdom and fine tuned means of judgment over other sentient Cities.

1 day, 3 hours, 42 minutes and 9 seconds after its discovery, after much singing and dancing (12 songs, 1 waltz and 2 tangos) unanimous support from the City's Politicians was given and it was ready for widespread use.

"Look at all we have done!" their words rang loud and clear. "Look at all we have become! City of Mann is a great City indeed! And how much more can we be! We will be known by our deeds and be seen for our treasure! With the Lord of lords by our side we are without measure!"

It was the same with the Silken Queen and the Humble High Priest.

"If God is with us then our glory knows no bounds!" they proclaimed. "And with God within our boundaries we have become Gods ourselves! Who among Sentient Citykind can stand before our majesty and noble might?! We are greater in every way!"

And Lord Pahnik? Well he was very much the same as before, but now he was backed by his friends, the Deacon of Dowting from Contrition and the Chief Gendarme of Gilt. Not new friends, they had been with him since the beginning, yet their supporters had grown at unprecedented speed. So as he spilled his fret-filled spiels, his heavy words carried much more weight.

The Will of the Feign

Now that Mann could see them, the problem of 'The Feign' was somewhat simpler than before. As armed with the knowledge that they were terrified of the Lord of lords they would run screaming at the mere mention of his name. So experts at hiding though they were, Mann set about clearing them from the City wherever he could. Yet it was not till BIA incident 827-373-838 that he was shown just how sneaky their sneakery could be.

The report of a sighting in a South Belongenham sent him rushing to the district to chase it out. Spotting a small crowd of friends and neighbors gathered in the front of the home, he had bellowed his maker's hallowed name as he approached.

It had been hiding quite sneakily in a sock drawer in a room upstairs. But upon hearing what it feared the most, it burst through the roof and fled, shrieking as it vanished into the air.

Satisfied with the outcome, Mann waved to the cheering crowd and turned to leave, till something caught his eye.

Among the huddle of his Citizen's happy faces, there was one who looked different to the rest. A handsome, well kempt fellow, with a fine tailored outfit to match.

Not happy like the rest, his face was pale and drawn—he was afraid. So watching him as he hurriedly pushed his way through the fray and moved away down the street, Mann followed.

Was he alright? Mann did not know.

"Excuse me," Mann called after him, rather concerned. "My little sir. Do you have a minute?"

At first it was as if he had not heard, so Mann called louder. But as he did, the man broke into a sprint.

"Hey!" he called again, "Excuse me! Hold on! I want to talk to you."

Something was amiss. Mann was confused. Did he not know who he was? If he did, his knowledge of his abilities were clearly misunderstood. No mere Citizen could even hope to outmatch him—let alone run away. He was the Spirit Ruler. This was his domain. So following the dashing fellow in a rather leisurely pace, he called one last time, before, as gently as he could manage, knocked him to the ground with a brush of his hand.

Yet then that he saw his face.

Set to apologize as he went to help him to his feet, he recoiled in horror. Like a mask, his features had somehow slipped, his eyes and nose as if made of melting wax. And beneath he saw it clear as day.[45] He was a Feign!

The Will of Mann

For all that Mann had been given in his new City, he could not seem to shake the old. With Citizens so terribly difficult and Politicians that seemed to have only a will for themselves, the revelation that the Feign could still hide within had puzzled him greatly. Was this how the new City was supposed to be?

45.
**'In Umbra Natus de Luce' (The Shadow Born of Light) Vol. II,
City di Gabriella Fortuna
ISBN 47-11-14/15**

". . . . . But Lord Mahvett! What if they see God for themselves? The radiance of the Maker is brighter by far than the brightest sun! If they see even a glimmer of his light—how can the light of the Feign compare?!"

"Compare? Ha! No, my Master Scoundrel. We can never hope to compare with the one who gave us life—but we don't have to. All we must convince them to do is to look the other way. We must tell them that their fairness is their liberty and their cleverness is their wealth. We must show them what they think they want and help them to imagine what they wish to see. We must be like mirrored glass, until all they see on all God's forms of good is their own reflections."

"But if they cannot see who we really are, who will they think us to be?"

"Who they *think* us to be does not matter! For all outside the light is in the shadow. As long as they are looking the other way, we can be monsters if they wish. For when the Sun is hidden from their eyes, it is the moon that gives them light! Then it will be I who is their God. I will be the shining one! And I will be their King!"

It had been some months since the City had been made new, yet as senior staff and Politicians shouted across the huge oval table and hammered on it with their fists, things did really not seem that different to before. And looking around the agitated yelling and red faced scowls, the new Situation Room was not what Mann had envisioned.

Rebuilt just across the street from the Temple a day or so after the one inside had been shut down, it was almost identical to the original, being fitted with the latest CMAC[46] technology while still retaining its practical layout and somber walnut tones.

Yet it was not the similarity in decor that bothered him. It was the atmosphere. And not just within the room either, but across most of the City itself.

On paper, all was going well. The statistics confirmed it. Crime was way down from this time last quarter, and only sixty three percent of the Idols destroyed had come back. It was true that some had come back stronger than before and there were a few new ones with new names, but the BIA was working on these and the overall progress was noticeable.

---

46. Described as *'Essential to every modern Sentient City environment'* by 'The Diatribe Digest', and receiving the IDGB's (Internal Dialogue Governance Board) Golden Cog award three years in a row, the Citizen Monitoring And Control system from CitiCorp is the number one way to keep your City happy and at peace.*

*According to happiness & peace as defined by CitiCorp ideals charter, sect. 4, part 26, item 7.

With the Lord of lords as Lord—the New Law and the light from the River was changing things,[47] and in general, the City was safer and more clean.

But as a torn toupee landed in his lap, Mann couldn't help but shake the feeling that something was off. And watching as the stenographer hurled a chair at a Councilman and Commander Strive got him in a chokehold before punching him in the eye, he couldn't help but wonder if something had gone wrong. As if maybe this was not how God had intended it to be.

But what more could he do? Outnumbered some thirty million to one by his Citizens, there was only so much time in a day. He had already delegated the work of calling them to the River to the BIA, but this had come with problems of its own.

Being Citizens themselves, they too were quick to forget. So as the golden words of the new law faded from their sight—whether by the sway of the Politicians or the Feign or simply on their own, it would not be long before they fell into their old mistakes.

He had tried to do it for them—the cleaning I mean—scrubbing for days at a time until their homes and streets glimmered with the new law. But the City was far too big. By the time he would finish for the day, the place where he had started

---

47. During a survey on 'Citizen happiness' conducted by the City of Mann statistician department, it was noted that Citizens born into the New City were much better at adopting the new way than Citizens who were natives of the Old.

This raised the question in academic circles of the possibility that time was a 'required' ingredient in adaptation to the New City, and that the death and birth cycle of its Citizens was a necessary process in order for the way of the New City to begin to become apparent.

that morning would already be thick with clutter and dirt. So as the months had gone on, he began to dismay.

What was the point? It seemed unfair. Where was the purpose in his failures and the provision in his lack of strength?

Was he being too critical? After all, most things were going to plan and in many ways the City had changed for the better—to some extent at least. And he was trying. He really was.

It was exhausting and far from restful—but with what he had to work with, what more could he do but his best? At the end of the day, his staff and advisors were only Citizens and still as silly and willful as the rest. And the Politicians? Willful was too mild a word. They seemed to live to undermine him. Always angling to paint themselves in the brightest light. And though they were not without purpose, he could not shake the feeling that his City was not entirely in his control.

It had only been two days earlier at work in Citicorp that their supporters had commandeered the City to belittle an Intern City in the lunchroom. And the day before that they did the same to call the poor fellow a fool. If Mann had known what was going to happen he would have—well, maybe he did know a little bit what was going on—but he did not know the boy was going to cry! It had been started by the Humble High Priest anyway! Preaching righteousness from the Temple steps, he had quickly drawn a crowd of Citizens to his favor and once Lord Pahnik and Judge Williams from Perditia joined him, there was no stopping them.

"He is nothing more than an insignificant stain!" they told the Citizens of the Intern. And stirring them into a fervid haze they declared him, "a threat nonetheless!" So with cries to keep the hapless lad in his place, they marched as one to Interfacer Command.

But the boy's poor despondent face. . .

Shaken from his troubled brooding as someone bumped his chair, his thoughts returned to the Situation room.

Not much more than a brawl in fancy dress and formal suits, it was chaos. Exchanging flailing blows, toppled furniture and scattered documents littered the floor. He flinched as the minister of justice was flung across the table. And as all the members of his Council seemed to scream nothing but the vicious and obscene, he could bear it no more. With a thundering blast of energy he unleashed his frustration.

"ENOUGH!!!!!" he roared, sending people tumbling head over heels by its force as window shattered and lights fell from the roof. "All of you!—Get back to your seats!!"

Struggling to calm the frustration in his chest, he took a deep breath, waiting for a moment to continue as the frightened members of his staff scampered back to their chairs.

"Ladies and Gentlemen of the Council," he growled, glaring around at their disheveled clothes and bruised faces. "Is this really what it looks like when we do our best?! This is supposed to be where we solve the problems of the City—not cause them!!"

Apart from a sniffle and an awkward shuffle of feet the room was silent. Either staring at the floor or wringing their hands, no one said a word.

"Now, before we start—I am not completely naive—if any of you are Feign; you have ten seconds to leave before I say the name of the Maker and turn you to dust."

With the creak of a chair from the back of the room, the Clerk of Works stood up and giving an appreciative little nod to Mann, headed out the door.

"Good," Mann continued as it clicked shut, "Anyone else?"

Letting the silence linger for a moment longer, he began. "Now, the rest of you. Put away your notepads and your pens.

Today I do not want the facts or the figures. I have seen them all. I just want to know the truth. As much as we may cover it in honey, I have seen our City. This cannot be how it was supposed to be! This cannot be what it looks like when we do our best? We are still harsh, still critical—sometimes I fear maybe even more than before! And when I look at you, I rarely see you think of anyone but yourselves. I just don't understand! How is it that even with the God of creation in our midst we are still making a mess? Please, someone tell me! How is it possible?. . . Ministers? Lords? Ladies?—Surely someone knows something? Can no one shed some light as to what is going on?!!"

Again, silence hovered over the room.

"Sire…" clearing his throat, the Commander straightened up in his seat. "Lord Mann," he said, "I— I apologize. I do. But—and I do not know how to say this so I mean no disrespect—but in all honesty my lord…some of us, were…we were happier with how it was before."

Furrowing his brow, Mann was puzzled. "Before?" he said. "Before what?"

"Before the New City my lord. Before the new way and the New City and the New Law."

With a collective gasp, a wave of whispers washed through the room as the words rang in Mann's ears.

"But— I don't understand. . ." he replied. "Have you forgotten from what we were saved? It was a nightmare Commander—a relentless march towards death! Even with our struggles, things are so much better now. Can't you see?"**48**

"I know, my lord. And for what has been done we are eternally grateful. But it is not that we have not seen…It is that we *have* seen—that is what is the matter. We have seen many things. Wonderful things, impossible things. Things too great to understand and things too wonderful to know. And that is just it. The Old City is all we have ever known. Far from perfect and destined for ruin, yes— But it was easy. We lived how we saw fit, with only our brightest desires and the best of Citykind to set the standard. But now, with these new eyes...The more we see, the more we see that we have fallen short. And I would ask you to forgive me sire, for if there is one thing I do know, it is that I cannot know. But of what I know of reality now—of the Creator,

---

48. "But Doctor Hammersmith!" Nurse Garnsworth gasped, as the clanking machine grew louder. "Surely you don't mean. . . a 'full' transformation!"

"I'm afraid I do Matilda," he replied, looking at the sleeping man's face through the glass hatch in the metal studded door. "I'm afraid I do." Pausing to take a thoughtful puff on his pipe, he continued. "But you needn't fret. This is what he was made for. Not only will he be improved, but he will become a whole new creature —the one he was meant to be. And besides my dear, you don't want to stop it now, do you? He's come so far. To stop now would be such a waste. I mean, think of yourself; before you were fully made, what transitions did you go through? In your creation you were scattered atoms, molecules, compost, cells. In any of those states, would you have said, 'no thank you, I'm perfectly comfortable being what I am. I don't want to be pulled apart and shaped into some new thing. Leave me alone.'"

"Well I suppose not," she replied.

"So you see, if we are to be changed, we are to be changed fully, —not in part. Only then can we become what we were made for. Anyway," he glanced at her with a cheeky twinkle in his eyes. I'm glad you didn't. I rather think you have been shaped quite well."

Taken from, 'Doctor Hammersmith Goes to Court', Aldridge LaPenn, (1956) ISBN 47-03-16/18

his purpose and his perfect provision—this new way and new law my lord. For us...it is impossible."

With an eruption of praise and angry shouts, the room exploded in a frenzy of heckles and applause.

"Bravo!" some acclaimed and, "Sacrilege!!" yelled others, while one befuddled aide mumbled, "I thought Mann was the Creator?" to himself.

Again, the floor rumbled as Mann shouted his command over the fray, "SILENCE!!!"

Waiting till the hush returned, his tone softened and he addressed the room, "Do you all feel this way? Surely the Commander does not speak for all of you?"

"Ladies and gentlemen!" Cutting through the uncomfortable quiet, the sound of the Humble High Priest's regal elegance rang out as he stood to his feet. "No one speaks for me but myself. But though I speak for myself; after great discussion, I speak on behalf of many more." With a courteous glance to either side he gestured to the Politicians seated around him. "Ladies and gentlemen, please, take heart! This new way is not impossible. What we are feeling now are merely the teething pains of youth. After all, if God is truly the all knowing and all powerful giver of all purpose and provision, what more could he expect? Was it not him who made the Citizens in their nature, and him who made us weak? Was it not him who permits the Feign to walk among us and even him, who at this very moment, permitted me to speak?"

The room rumbled with approval, "Hear, hear!"

"So what do you say then Rupert?" Mann asked. "What do you suggest we do?"

Pausing first for dramatic effect, the High Priest continued, "My lord; members of the council; my brothers and sisters...We know now of God and his wonderful ways, and for this we give thanks. We know now of his marvelous power and we are grateful. But we also know now, that because we were worthy, that it is our humble City in whom the Lord of lords has come to live! Not one of the wealthy Cities of Angelo, or even the religious Cities of Trent—but City of Mann!!"

As a round of cheer reverberated to his predication he resumed his impassioned words.

"My friends! It is us who the God of creation has given the mantle! The new way is not impossible—with him by our side we are kings! We are the arbiters of the new standard. So not only is it possible, it is so! With him by our side we are to be the gods of our fate and nothing can stand in our way!!"

In a thunder of euphoria, the room exploded in exultation and cheer. Yet as it mixed with screams of outrage from those who disagreed, it was only a moment before it descended back into a tangle of violence.

As the first airborne bottle hit its target with a pained yelp, through the vicious shrieks of ministers and politicians Mann sighed, closing his eyes as he buried his head in his hands.

"Maybe we should ask for help!"

Barely audible through the squabble, Mann cocked his head as a familiar little voice called out. Then he heard it again, "Excuse me! I'd like to say something!"

"Who said that?!" Mann exclaimed, straining to hear. "Everyone quiet!!"

As the tumultuous volume subsided, Mann scanned the battered members of his establishment with concern. "Gibald?"

"Yes my lord?" replied the voice from the back.

"Is that you?"

"Yes my lord."

And it was. The crowd parting to his squeaky little sound, there he was, looking rather nervous with his hand raised above his head. "My apologies, my lord. Would it be alright for me to speak?"

"Of course," Mann replied with a smile, always pleased to see his friend. "You should not be back there. You should be here by my side."

"Thank you sire. I didn't want to be any bother, but I—" Stopping short, he surveyed the scornful gaze of the battered aristocracy whispering amongst themselves. "I was just. . ."

"Do not mind them little one. They are just wind—a distraction. My ear is always yours. What is it that you wish to say?"

"Thank you, sire," he stuttered. "I...I was just thinking that for all our plans and all our struggles—and I do not mean to be rude my lord, to you, or to any of you lords and ladies greater than me. But how can we say that our circumstance is impossible or say that it should be by our plans that we dictate God's thoughts? Surely if the Lord of lords is perfect purpose and perfect provision, has not all of what is needed for good already been done? Do we say we add to it because it is lacking, or change it because it is wrong? We do not. We cannot. All has been given and all has been done. Every path to his perfect will has already been laid.**49** If there is any knowledge among you of who God really is, you would see that it *could* not be any other way! So how can we speak as if we comprehend his purpose or act on his behalf as if we know his plans? Surely all we ever need in all things, is to ask him what he wants?"

Gibald was not wrong. And as a hushed symphony of startled whispers trembled from the lips of his council, Mann mused his humble words. Truth be told, for as much as he liked to think he knew what it was that he was to do, he did not and even if he did, he had no idea how to do it. So taking a deep breath, he left the Situation room far behind, and went in search of his maker.

---

49.   **The Ballad of the Humble Traveler, Anonymous.**
(ISBN 59-04-10/20-03-05/08)

Flowers aflutter from 'round my face, I hang here from my tree.
It really is a long way down, what is your will for me?

Black clouds are a yonder, leaves twinkling in the breeze.
If it be your will for me, I'll hold fast to stem with ease.

The roar of tempest growing, I quake but hear your voice,
If it be your will, strong wind, your will is still my choice.

Pulled from where you shaped me, you take me from my branch,
If the mud is what you will to be, then here I do my dance.

The driving rain it beats me so, yet hark, I hear a squeak,
You've sent a feathered creature, to save me in its beak!

Sat here in its innards, this place is dark and foul,
Yet for good your will will always be, so in glee I wonder how.

Released with stinking ardor, and most unpleasant sound,
I laugh for every wondrous gift, as I hurtle to the ground.

Laid to rest in fertile soil, I truly have been freed,
As I know your will is willed to be, so I give my thanks to thee.

Chapter 18

A MORE EXCELLENT WAY

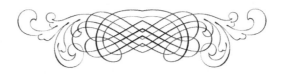

F alling to his knees before the Lord of lords in the Temple, Mann asked for help.

And it was there, in that quiet place, that purpose was fulfilled. God heard and God answered.

Taken by the hand, Mann was raised to his feet. There was still much more to learn.

The Politicians were to be taken from power. The Biters were to be removed. There were even hidden rooms in the Temple that had never been cleaned!

But first, he was to go to the River to drink. So requesting only that he hold tight, the Lord of lords led the way.

Then, rising rapidly to new heights, he was taken upward into the sky. He had never left his world, yet as it disappeared below, he saw it like he had never seen before. The Plains of Eudamonia to the west and to the north, the Valleys of the Phree. Beneath, the metropolis of Epicurea on the Atraxian coast, nestled in the twinkling Sea.

Faster and faster still as he whipped through a billowing cloud he caught his breath as looking back he saw himself. His home; his life; his empire. His City of Mann. His him. The he who he is, the he who he was. All he had ever known and all who he had ever been. But now so small. So strange. A mere circle, a vanishing dot. And he was not alone. There were so many, he could see them all. Thousands of them—tens of thousands—circles and dots just like him, unaware of the pattern that they formed, each a delicate, purposed note of the symphony of Citykind.

Then, there was silence—just as there was for me—as he reached the frigid vacuum of space. And as he watched the planet of his kind turn, it danced with the swirling shapes of storms and rains that dappled its surface.

It was in this way that I too saw the blaze of the sun for myself. Given eyes to see, I too was shown the moons that bathed beneath its light, passing strange planets of every type awash with blanched and vivid colors. Shown the nebulae and galaxy I saw the wonders of the celestial bloom, as hurtling past exploding stars and stellar surge I moved at terrifying speed. Until, as matter and time began to bend and shake and the walls of my dimension collapsed— finally, in a blinding flash, I was there.

Its lush pastures and mighty oceans brushed in emerald and sapphire—Earth. The home of mankind.

It was here, alas, that I gave spoil to the moment. Sneezing on some cosmic dust, I apologized to the Lord as I wiped my nose with my sleeve. But as he said 'no fear', there was more to be seen. For here was the home to his weakest.

Humans, as I have expressed, were very strange indeed. Why God had made such a contradiction to his power and perfection was a mystery to me, as it was indeed to Mann.

Theirs was a picture of all that lacked. So vulnerable and foolish, they were so easy to confuse. Squishy in a way most disturbing, he felt sorry for them too. Compared to the others of God's sentient kinds, they were hopeless—hapless. Yet, as he held tight to the one who guided him, he saw that nothing was for naught. For in all that they lacked, as with all things, there was perfect purpose and provision. And theirs was to be a greater purpose than any else.

For from the fruitless soil of their kind, God would sow a single Seed, and from it bring the finest of all his fruits. And in all the futility that God had subjected his creation, it was through them, humanity, that the fullness of his love would be revealed.

So, as Mann was formed since the start, he remained; in the hand of perfect provision. Day gave way to night and night gave way to day. Light gave life, and darkness took the sight of those who claimed to see. Greed and kindness rose like the tides. A bird was smashed on the rocks, as another, who cried, was lifted by a gentle wind. Invention washed discomfort clean as war swept their globe like burning waves. Babies were born. Books were read. The living laughed and the living died. The dead slept, and a cat got stuck up a tree. The injured found love and lovers found hate. And as the countless hosts of the realms watched it all with eager longing for what was to be, Mann was at peace.

The End

Printed in Great Britain
by Amazon

48821585R00101